Heaven is to Your Left -

An LGBT Historical Fiction:

Juliana Series: Book 4
(1956)

by
Vanda

Sans Merci Press

Cover Design: Ann McMan

Edited by: Deborah Dove at Polgarus Studio

Library of Congress Number: 2018912452

FREE

Want something for nothing?

**Details
at the back of the
book**

PRAISE FOR THE JULIANA SERIES

In Praise of The Juliana Series (Books 1, 2 & 3)

"(Juliana) captures the fear, excitement, and eroticism of a young lesbian's awakening in the 1940s." (*Kirkus Reviews*)

"Vanda creates a historical novel about a time period in which we know very little about queerness--WWII... Vanda's narratives, prowess of timely language and setting and character development lend a poignant message: to be queer was to be anti-American." -- July Westhale (**Lambda Literary Review**)

"From the first page, I felt I was walking on the streets of 1940s New York. At times funny, enlightening, sensual, *Juliana* tells a story that is rarely told. --Donna Spector, *The Candle of God, The Woman Who Married Herself.*

"This novel (*Olympus Nights on the Square*) clearly shows how far women's rights and the LGBT community have come. I have a greater appreciation for all of those men and women who have fought for our rights to live and love out loud. I believe it is important for the LGBT community to be reminded of the struggles and sacrifices that have brought us to where we are today. Why is this important? It is important for someone like myself because I live in a country where my love is illegal and the LGBT community in the Caribbean is often sidelined and our rights are ignored. Therefore, reading this story has showed me that it is possible to see light at the end of a very dark tunnel. Our Caribbean LGBT activists are not giving up, and it gives me some hope that someday I may have the opportunity to say that my country said YES! to love and freedom for all." (**The Lesbian Review**, 2/11/18)

Vanda delivers another phenomenal piece to the Juliana series! The characters I've grown to love have evolved into even bigger, brighter, beautiful people and new characters are added to the mix whom I now love just as much as the original. In this book, Al is going through a massive internal struggle. She is on the fence about whether or not she is a lesbian, one of "them", which is interesting to see and I think it's something all of us could relate to. I was proud when Al declared herself gay because finally she isn't ashamed of who she is. There were some powerful words and struggles in this book and again is a perfect period piece. Not only do we get a glimpse into the lives of post-WWII LGBT characters, we also are reminded how tough it was to be a woman back then. Al turns into a career-oriented college graduate, which of course is a tough thing to be in that time. I eagerly look forward to the next additions to the Juliana series. If you've read Juliana, read Olympus as well! If you haven't read Juliana, well, what are you doing with your life?! (**Amanda Beilfuss**)

"In this way, *Olympus Nights* can be seen as a lesbian coming-of-age story with all the recognizable dangers present in the past that a more modern audience can still feel. Yet, even though the story really is centered on the women, the men in Al's life also have important roles to play. We're treated to historical glimpses of stars, such as Walter Winchell, Liberace, and Mayor O'Dwyer; and squirm with Max, Al's mentor and ally, and Marty, a former soldier and aspiring actor, as they struggle to be their true selves. In every chapter, Vanda highlights the political climate of the times and brings forth a wealth of information describing the anti-Gay, anti-People of Color, anti-Communist, anti-Jew, and anti-Woman policies in New York City and America, during that decade."(**An Amazon Customer**)

"I just finished *Juliana* and *Olympus Nights* and cannot wait to start *Paris Adrift*. These are some of the most amazing and important books that I have read in a good while. I am a fan of LesFic stories, but this is much more than that. These stories have to be told and appreciated. Thank you for all the work and research that was put into these stories. It's much appreciated." (**An Amazon Customer**)

"Romance enveloped in a time period most of us could not imagine struggling through. Reading this series has made me so grateful to those that fought the good fight before us, and grateful this author does not let us forget their struggle." (**An Amazon Customer**)

Our descent was a little rocky. The plane bucked us in our seats. The captain had warned us there'd be some slight turbulence on our way down; it'd begun to snow in New York. I looked down at my lap. I had a rolled-up copy of the *Pan Am Clipper* magazine in my hands and I was choking it. Not because of the turbulence, but because of what awaited Juliana and me in New York.

All during the flight, Jule and I had hardly uttered a word to each other, just the few pleasantries strangers might exchange on an airplane. Both of us lost, I suspect, in our fears of what would come next. Every time I started to doze off, I saw Schuyler's face grinning at me and it'd jar me awake. After he'd forced Juliana to sign that contract to do the Broadway musical, he pretty much left us alone. Of course, to an outsider, being "forced" to star in a Broadway musical wouldn't seem like such a terrible thing, but . . . One night a day or so after she'd signed that contract, we were sleeping in my room. The whole business had brought us closer together and she didn't worry anymore about us turning into Shirl and Mercy, our two women friends who lived together. We'd taken to sleeping in my bed every night, even though her bed, in the larger room, was bigger. One night I was jarred awake by her thrashing in her sleep. I raised myself up on my elbow. "Jule," I whispered and lightly touched her shoulder. She shook herself awake and lay there, staring at the ceiling. "Are you okay?" I asked.

"Yes. Yes," she said. "A dream. Just a . . ." She threw her legs over the side of the bed, her fingernails gripping the edge of the mattress.

"I'll get you a glass of water." I ran into the bathroom and came back with the water. She took the glass into her two hands but didn't drink; she just stared into it as if she were waiting for a goldfish to poke its head out. She slid off the bed and put the glass on the end table. "Al, I—

I . . . You're so much braver than I am. I . . ." She turned to face me.

"What is it?" I asked

"I—I can't do it. I can't. I'm finished." She walked over to the French windows, peering past the curtains.

"You can do it, hon. You are so talented. You just need to *believe* in your talent. That's what I'm here for. To keep reminding you."

"When I was up on that stage two years ago and people walked out —those were the kindest ones. Others laughed and booed. I think I died on that stage then, or felt like it. The critics said awful things. Some were even the critics who had praised me in the clubs, but they turned on me and—"

"Jule, that happened because you weren't singing. The play was a drama." I wished I could remind her it was Richard who had signed her for that horribly bad play. It wasn't just her; even an experienced thespian would have had a tough time keeping that bomb afloat. "Jule, there was no music. You had no experience and no training in that sort of thing. It's not what you do. It's not what you're a genius at. This time you'll be singing, and the audience'll see the real you."

"I can't." She fluffed her hair and moved away from the window. "Schuyler is going to ruin me. He's going to publicize that I'm a . . . a . . ." Her face turned paler than usual.

"We won't give him the chance to do that."

She turned to me. "Aren't you scared? If our relationship comes out, he'll ruin your life too. Max will have to fire you. You won't get another job. You're not scared I'll flop and ruin your life too?"

"I'm scared, yeah, but I know you can do it, so in another way I'm not scared."

"Get me out of this."

"What? But you signed the contract. That's what Max advised you to do. He also advised you to trust *me*."

"And I do. Please don't think I don't." She put her hands together as if she were praying and nodded them at me. "It's me I don't trust."

"That's your mother talking. Always making you feel like you weren't measuring up to *her* dream. You've already surpassed her."

"You can get me out of it. I know you can. Then I can go back to singing in the clubs. Forget about Broadway. That was my original plan. All you have to do is get me out of that contract and make Schuyler keep his mouth shut."

"That's all, huh? Jule, do you hear what you're asking me? Why would Schuyler do that for me?"

"He would, he would. You have a way with people. You can make things work."

"Jule, I'm not Max. And even Max couldn't think of a way around this except by signing that contract. I'm also not a lawyer. And if we did take him to court, the whole thing would come out. All over the world. Doing that play is the only way out of this."

"No, it can't be. It can't be." She wrung her hands and paced. "No, there must be some other way."

I gripped her shoulders to stop all that movement. "Easy, hon." I wrapped my arms around her and brought her close to me. She folded her arms around my waist and laid her head on my shoulder. I reached up to pat her head.

"You can fix this. I know you can," she said.

No matter how much I thought and thought, I couldn't come up with a plan. I'd talk to Max again when we got home.

The plane dipped down, and my stomach turned over. I feared that if we didn't land soon I'd need the white throw-up bag that was stuffed into the back pocket of the seat in front of me. I leaned near Juliana, joining her in looking out the window. "Maybe it'd be better if we didn't make it," she whispered to the clouds beyond the glass.

"You're kidding, aren't you?" I said, a bit horrified.

"Yes. I think."

My ears began to pop and I furiously swallowed. I hated my ears doing that. "You want a stick of gum?" Juliana asked.

"Please."

She reached into her alligator handbag and took out an open package of spearmint. She shook out one for each of us. I leaned back in my seat, chewing wildly.

My chewing slowed when I recalled the time after Jule had first begged me to get her out of the contract. I couldn't bear to see her in such pain, so I went to Schuyler's Pigalle office. Jule was off in the provinces working, so she didn't know. I made my way through the odd carnival sights of Pigalle: the bearded ladies, the ladies who stripped in the street, the lady with the cobra crawling up her almost nude body. I entered a dark cabaret, not yet open for business. A blonde woman stood on a small stage wearing nothing but a silver triangle covering her privates. I was shocked to find myself getting aroused. How many topless and near-naked ladies had I seen on this trip? I think it had something to do with that silver triangle. In the corner, a female impersonator sat at a table smoking, coughing, and drinking from a highball glass. She wore a loose-fitting pink dress; it looked a lot like the housedresses my mother used to wear. Her bright red lipstick was smeared away from the edges of her mouth and much of it was pressed onto the edge of her glass. "Excuse me, ma'am," I said. Her tired eyes, heavy with overdone turquoise eye shadow, peered up at me from under her wide-brimmed hat. "English?" I asked, hoping. She shook her head no. "Schuyler?" I asked. She pointed her pinky, still wrapped around the glass, at the opposite wall. I went over to the wall and turned down the hallway. There at the end near a closed door stood Schuyler, leaning on a broom, an apron over his unbuttoned suit jacket. He sure didn't look terribly intimidating dressed like that. I had a chance with him. "Schuyler!" I commanded.

He snapped to attention like a soldier, then seeing it was me, his body slumped. "What are *you* doing here?"

"I'm here, that's all. I want to talk. But it doesn't look like you're the kind of guy who'd have an office available."

"Oh yeah? You'll see." He sounded like a child daring me. He tore the apron off and kicked the door next to him open. "In!"

I marched in, giving him my most lethal stare as I passed. Inside there was an empty desk, a couple of chairs, and a floor that was a dusty mess. The one window to the side of the desk looked as if it hadn't been washed in months it was so caked with gunk. There was nothing on the wall except for a large painting directly behind Schuyler's desk chair. Not exactly the office of an executive or powerful producer. He threw off his apron, tightened his tie, spat on his hands, and ran his palms over the top of his head, apparently engaged in some type of grooming ritual. To impress me? He sat down.

I sat on the opposite side of the empty desk, staring at the "art-work" hanging behind him. A thickly painted woman lay on her bed in a can-can outfit. Her legs were parted, so you could see she wasn't wearing any underwear. I found it disgusting, but it was something I'd expect to find in Schuyler's office. Except—I'd seen this same painting in other offices I'd visited in Paris. The French's rules of decorum between the sexes are quite different from America's rules. This sort of thing would never be permitted in the US. It could even get you arrested.

"So, what is it you want?" Schuyler asked. "I didn't expect to see you again until we all got back to New York."

"You've got to let Juliana out of that contract."

"Ha! She signed it. She's mine."

"But don't you see?" I leaned on his desk and looked into his eyes. "If you force her, she could fall apart. You'll be ruining your own investment. I can get you Lili Donovan. But first you've got to tear up that contract." I sat back in my chair. "You know how good Lili is. On the ship you said you were interested. She's already got a worldwide reputation."

He leaned back in his chair. "Hmm, you're right. Lili's good, but very different from Juliana."

"I can get her to do it like Juliana."

He was silent a moment, watching me. My eyes wouldn't leave his. I had to win this. He picked up a few pieces of paper from his desk and began slowly ripping them up. Could that be the contract? Had I gotten through to him? He let the pieces sprinkle through his fingers and fall onto the desktop. I quickly ran through Lili's schedule. Was she even free to do this? She had to be, even if I had to call in a lot of favors.

"You're a pretty tough girl, aren't you?" he said. "You can do anything."

"I *can* get Lili. She's *my* client. Just rip up Juliana's contract and give me the pieces and I'll—"

"You'll make everything all right. Won't you? All I have to do is rip up this contract." He held up some bulky folded papers. That must be it—the contract. If I could only reach out and grab it . . . "Oh, yes, I'll just do that. I'll rip this right up." He tore the folded piece to bits. "My main investor will only do the show with Juliana."

"Who is he? I'll convince him to do it with Lili."

"You really are something, missy, aren't you? My investor only wants Juliana. I told you that on the ship."

"Then dump him. You'll be able to raise the money with Lili."

"Hmm? Now, that's an interesting proposition. You want me to take the best deal I've ever had, one that's guaranteed, and throw it in the toilet on your say so." He started to laugh as he tore up more paper and threw it around the room. He fell out of his seat with laughter. His laughter turned ugly; it was the growl of a wild animal. He rolled around on the floor, his joy sounding more like agony.

I stood over him. "Schuyler!" I shouted. "Stop this and listen to me." His body jackknifed, almost knocking me to the ground. I jumped out of the way in time. His laughter and jerky movements grew wilder and wilder. It seemed like he was having some kind of fit. He wouldn't stop, so I ran from the place.

"We're going to have to be more careful than we ever have," Juliana said softly. "We can't afford even the slightest slip-up or Schuyler will ruin both our lives."

"I know," I said. Her perfume surrounded me with the faint scent of lemons, and I wanted to reach out and . . . I couldn't do that. The most innocent touch would now be more suspect than ever. But what if she really couldn't do it? What if she got so scared she froze and really did flop? What would Schuyler do to us then? No, don't think like that. She can do it. She will do it. She'll make his show a hit; he'll get the big reputation he wants, outdo his father, and then leave us alone.

The pilot made a fairly smooth landing with only a few more bumps and knocks before we were down and coasting toward the area where we'd exit. My legs were stiff from sitting there for nine hours.

Standing at the top of the steps near the stewardess, watching the people below gripping their winter coats as they pushed through the glass doors eager to meet their loved ones, was like watching a silent black-and-white movie in slow motion. A steady flurry of white flakes hit the black pavement and melted, no sound; people dressed in gray moved their mouths, no sound. My terror was shutting out all sound, all color, and even normal movement. Then I saw Max in his London Fog and fedora looking as dapper as ever, and the world's color rushed back in.

"There he is," I said to Juliana as we started down the steps.

"Where?" she asked, holding onto her wide-brimmed hat so it didn't fly into the wind. I thought I heard excitement in her voice. Or was that relief?

"There. Leaning against the building where all those people are waiting behind the rope, waving and yelling."

"No, I don't . . . Oh, yes. Yes. There he is."

Yes, I thought, there he is. He'll save us from Schuyler.

Workmen in blue shirts and pants bumped into each other trying to get a good look at her. Who could blame them? She was breathtaking in her Jacques Fath double-breasted green suit and mink jacket. I held my fox stole tighter around my shoulders; it was cold. Daylight was fading fast into January's early darkness. Snow drifted down onto our heads.

We stepped onto the asphalt and pushed past the crowds grabbing for loved ones as they hurried away from snow and cold into the reception area. Max, who'd been leaning against the wall smoking a cigarette in his holder, straightened up as we approached. I ran to him and threw my arms around his neck. He pulled me close. "You're home, kid. You're finally home." His Clark Gable mustache wiggled up and down like maybe he was trying not to cry.

"So, you missed me, huh? You really missed me?"

"Of course, I did. You left me with two—*two* clubs to run all by myself."

"And that's the *only* reason?"

"What other reason could there be?" He grinned, tapping me on the head. He gently swept snow from the top of my flat hat with the side of his hand. Then, looking closer, he said, "Did you get your hair cut?"

"Yup!" I said, ripping my hat off. "Jule got it for me."

"She did?"

He looked over my head at Juliana. "Well, if *she* approves, it must be all right."

"And how exactly do you mean that, Max?" Juliana said stiffly.

Walking past me toward Juliana, he said, "Only in the best possible way, dear. Welcome home."

"Hello, Max." I heard a slight quiver in her voice as she hurried to slide her black gloves off; she placed them in her handbag and took out a match to light a Galois. The snow immediately dampened the match.

"Allow me," Max said, pulling a lighter from his coat pocket and flicking it at her cigarette.

"Thank you." She took a puff. She only smoked when she was nervous or upset.

"It's good to see you," Max said.

"Is it?" she said, still withholding any warm feelings.

"Yes, Juliana. It is," Max said.

They sighed simultaneously, a sigh that perhaps signaled the end of sixteen years of exhausting animosity. The two of them had hardly spoken to each other in all that time. Despite the different rumors about why, no one knew for sure. Some said it was because Juliana chose Richard over Max to manage her career; others said it was because they'd fallen in love but couldn't do much about it, both being gay. Still others insisted that Max got mad because Juliana married Richard, making her life a lie and forcing Richard to unknowingly participate in it.

From a distance, I saw Richard pushing his way through the crowds to get to us. For a chubby little guy, he certainly could weave his way through a crowd. And always polite. That's one thing you could say about Richard. He was always polite. He wore a thick gray overcoat, which made him look chubbier than he really was, and a fedora pressed way down on his head. He reached us and threw his arms around his wife. "Julie, my girl, you're home, you're home." Juliana extended her cheek and Richard kissed it. "It's only a little bit of snow," Richard said. "You would've thought it was a big storm the way everything is gummed up on the highway. The traffic just wouldn't move. Sorry I'm late." He put another kiss on her cheek.

"You're not late, honey," Juliana assured him. "We just got here."

She called him honey. I'd never heard her do that before.

"Max," Juliana began, "I believe you've met my husband, Richard."

"Yes." Max extended his hand. "It's been a long time. Good to see you, Richard."

I wondered how hard that was for Max.

"Who expected this snow?" Richard said, taking Max's hand.

"Well, it *is* January," Max said.

"Julie, you must be frozen," Richard said.

"A little cold around the legs, yes," she said. "But this jacket keeps the rest of me warm."

"Always like to dress my girl in the warmest. Max, let's get the girls inside."

Max and Richard guided Juliana and I toward the door. Max stopped, looking closely at Juliana, so we all stopped. "Did you cut off *your* hair too?"

"Well, as a matter of fact, I did." She took off her hat.

"Julie!" Richard gasped.

"What? It's very French. All the rage in Paris."

"Yes, but . . . Your beautiful long hair . . ."

"Old-fashioned, Richard. I need to keep up-to-date."

"Well, I-I suppose, but . . ." He looked like he might cry.

"Well, *I* like it," Max announced. "Very modern."

"Thank you." Jule nodded at Max.

"Very attractive, dear," Richard choked out.

As we moved closer to the door, Richard grabbed my shoulder and pulled me back. "What do *you* think, Al?"

"Me? I love it. Don't worry, Richard, you'll get used to it." I couldn't blame Richard for being shocked. I was ready to kill her the first time I saw she'd had her signature black tresses cut off. But after I got over the shock, I had to admit the style looked great. "Richard, it's working like gangbusters for Ava Garner, so why not Jule? It's very French. Perfect for her."

"Okay. If *you* say so, Al. You're the one who knows."

Max helped Juliana put her hat back on. As we entered into the airport lounge, flash cameras instantly blinked in Juliana's face. She squinted and covered her eyes. Max took her arm, guiding her through a pressing crowd. "Okay, easy boys."

"Did you set this up?" Juliana asked Max.

"Not me. I had a quiet homecoming planned at my place."

"Al?" Max asked.

"No."

I looked at Richard.

"Don't jump on *me*," Richard said. "*I* didn't plan it."

I looked around the crowded room of autograph seekers trying to get close to her. A couple of reporters from small unimportant TV stations like channel five and nine were pressing toward her with microphones. Juliana was known in the nightclub circuit, but she wasn't Frank Sinatra or Jimmy Durante so why were they flocking around her? Something was wrong. Ordinarily, this would thrill me, but . . . Then I saw . . . Way in the back. Schuyler.

"Oh, Miss Juliana, I just love you," a pimply-faced teenage girl gushed as she pushed her autograph book into Juliana's stomach. She wore one of those popular poodle skirts with a raised flamingo on the front. "I have all of your records, and when I heard you were going to be starring on Broadway I thought I'd perish. Just perish. Could you make it out to 'Candy'?"

"All right, Candy," Juliana said with her well-practiced smile of patience for clumsy young people. As she handed Candy back her book, she gave me a look that I read as, "What is this?"

I turned to Richard. "You didn't plan it, but you *knew* about it, didn't you?"

"Well, uh, Dan said this would be good for the show and Julie's career and as her manager—"

"Why didn't you at least wire me?"

"Dan wanted to keep it a secret.

"Oh, did *Dan?* You and *Dan* wanted to keep it a secret from me? Thanks, Richard, thanks a lot. And where was *Dan* when your mother got sick and you couldn't go to Paris. I just got back from a grueling trip, running the whole show, doing *your* job, Mr. *Manager* and you—"

"You're right. You are completely right. I should've told you. I wasn't thinking, but you're completely right."

"I sure the heck am, and it better not happen again. I want to know *everything* that's happening or is about to happen with Juliana's career. That's our deal. *I* run the show."

"Yes. Yes, of course. I'm sorry. I never meant to—"

"Okay." I reined in my anger, some of it very real, but some of it put on to make sure Richard didn't think he would ever really be in control of Jule's career. Schuyler was manipulating us already and we hadn't even been home five minutes.

"It's okay," I said again to Richard, who was looking upset. I couldn't take this out on him. He only wanted what was best for Juliana. He didn't know the kind of strain she was under. He must *never* know that. I sidled over to Max, who stood against the wall, smoking.

"Max?"

"Yes?"

"Aren't you going to do something?"

"About what? Disperse a crowd that's nuts for her? Really, Al, you're a better businesswoman than that."

"She's exhausted. And this is just another one of Schuyler's tricks to own her. I bet more than half these people don't even know who she is."

"But tomorrow morning they will; *everyone* will."

"It's a publicity stunt."

"A damn good one." He left me to stand by Juliana's side, making sure he was in some of those pictures. He was always doing what was good for business.

Furious, I pushed through the crowds, ducking the flashbulbs popping all around, trying to get to Schuyler. This sort of thing could raise the public's expectations of her sky high, which would make it all that much harder to please them. He was setting her up for a gigantic fall.

I was charging through the bottleneck of people when I tripped over the leg of someone's home-movie-camera tripod and almost fell into Schuyler's arms.

"What is this?" I yelled over the din.

He tightened his tie and brushed back a clump of black hair from his forehead. "PR for the show, of course." He held both of his hands in the air, forming an invisible newspaper headline: "BROADWAY STAR RETURNS TO THE GOOD OL' US OF A. Or "JULIANA CONQUERS PARIS." You didn't think I'd miss this opportunity, did you? *The Herald* and *Daily Mirror* are going to have something on it tomorrow."

"She *isn't* a Broadway star."

"Yet."

"Yet. Do you have any idea what incredible stress you are putting on her?"

"I'm merely putting an idea into the minds of her future fans. This'll make it easier for her to soar once she's actually on Broadway."

"Or give her a greater fall. The New York critics are going to be hungry for a second fall after a hullaballoo like this. They'll be chomping at the bit to humiliate her for even having the audacity to attempt a second Broadway show after her last flop. You should've consulted me first."

"I consulted her manager." He bent close to me and whispered with an ugly grin, "You're just her bull dyke." He straightened up. "She looks lovely, doesn't she? Signing those autographs. A glamorous Broadway star. That's what *I'm* doing for her."

She did look lovely. And he *was* the one doing it for her, not me. My heart was slowly sliding into my stomach. I watched as Juliana signed another young girl's autograph book and then a teenaged boy's. I remembered the young girl I'd been the first time I met her in person. It was in her dressing room after a show. She sat at her vanity, sliding a stocking down one of her legs. I stood there foolishly holding out my program toward her, strange, unfamiliar feelings jumping up and down inside me.

"Did you want me to sign that?" she asked

"Oh, yes, would you?" I gushed.

"No," she said, sliding down the second stocking. I wanted to run out of that room and hide. "I have a feeling," she continued, padding across the floor to her Japanese screen, "you and I are going to know each other for a long time. I'll sign that when we know each other better, when it will mean something." That was almost sixteen years ago.

I saved and protected that program through all the passing days, waiting for the time when it would be signed. When that day finally arrived—her opening at the Copa—she couldn't sign it. It was *too* hard for her to express her feelings to me on a program. I guess we got to know each other too well. I'd carefully preserved that unsigned program in saran wrap and kept it in my night table drawer next to my bed. But the memories—the memories of that unsigned program—those I would keep inside me forever.

CHAPTER TWO

The snow that started the previous night at the airport continued. It wasn't putting any brakes on New York City traffic, but it sure was slowing things down a bit. I entered the Haven. The orchestra was playing the preshow music; I stomped my feet on the "Welcome to the Haven" doormat and hopped to the lobby wall. I tore off my too-tight galoshes. Luckily, the cab driver had pulled right up to the curb, so my dark green Madeleine de Rauch gown made with honest-to-goodness Robert Perrier silk from Paris didn't get dragged through the slush. My fox stole was falling off one shoulder, and my hat was a little dented from a snowball some brat threw at me from across the street. I felt a little bedraggled, but when I checked my parts, everything seemed to be in the right place. I took my heels out of the felt bag I carried and dumped my galoshes inside.

I straightened up when I heard Marty's soft baritone drifting into the lobby. I thought he was still in Hollywood learning to ride a horse. He was singing "Dancing in the Dark," and I pictured the dance floor crowded with couples in each other's arms. I was home. I had a momentary imagining of Juliana and me dancing under the Haven's blue dome like we had at Chez Moune in Paris.

I stood at the entrance to our main dining room. It looked a little empty for the hour; only a few sat at the round tables on the edge having a pre-show dinner. The snow, I guessed.

A couple—he in a tux, she in a gown and stole—rushed past me heading to the coat check booth. He helped her slip out of her wrap. I stopped short, only able to see Bertha's hands reaching for their things from the coat check booth. I took a deep breath and hurried toward my office. "Hi," Bertha said cheerfully as I walked past her booth. I kept walking. "Welcome home," she yelled after me. "We missed you." I needed to make it into my office before she found some reason to follow me and do some ridiculous...

She stepped in front of me and started dusting the rug in front of my office door. "Uh, Bertha, please. That isn't necessary." She had to be the one who was in cahoots with Schuyler. The one who told him about Juliana and me. But how would she know? She was always in my office dusting or straightening something, even when I told her not to. Was there anything in there that would give us away?

"Please, Bertha! Stop sweeping. I want to get into my office."

"Oh, yes, of course," she said, backing up. She slid the broom across the rug past my feet, bowing all the way back to her coat check booth.

Disgusted, I unlocked my door, shoved it open, threw my wrap and my navy blue hat onto my office chair without bothering with the light, and headed toward the dining room, wondering if Juliana had arrived yet.

Max, in his tuxedo, dashed about giving orders to the waiters and busboys; he frantically straightened ashtrays that didn't need straightening and poked at the yellow roses in the crystal vases in the center of the tables. He sure was going all out for Juliana's first visit to his Swing Street club. It was like he was expecting the new queen of England. I imagined he considered Juliana in the same vein and, well, she did have a lord for a father. I suppose that meant technically she *was* Lady Juliana. She would've hit me in the head if I ever called her that.

Marty's mellow baritone filled the room while a few couples danced on the shiny dance floor surrounding the stage. I decided I should go over and try to settle Max down so he didn't collapse, but before I got there Lucille was already at his side, pulling him into a chair. She signaled for the bartender to bring him a glass of water. *She* certainly was efficient. Maybe too efficient. I approached them hesitantly, aware of the swish of my flared crinoline gown.

"Al!" Lucille exclaimed, jumping up and down. "You're here, you're here!" She threw her arms around me, her own flared gown crinkling into mine. We both wore sleeveless dresses so her bare flesh brushed against mine. I half-heartedly hugged her back, wanting to be free of touching flesh that might have cut into mine in the worst possible way. I managed a smile, as one does in those moments, and stepped back from her. But . . . could *she* be the one who betrayed us? Was she the one working with Schuyler? Did she even *know* about Juliana and me?

"Look at you!" Lucille exclaimed. "Paris has certainly been good to you. Your hair."

She touched the side of my brushed back short hair with the fingers of her pink gloves.

"Your hair is so gone, man. Like real gone."

It was apparent that while I was away, Lucille had spent entirely too much time with the musicians.

I walked over to Max, who was slumped in a chair near a center table. He looked exhausted. "Don't worry, Max," I said. "She's gonna love this place."

"You really think so?"

"Of course. I'm the one who made it what it is."

"After *I* trained you. But you did it, kid, you really did. And *then*, you left me alone with it."

"Alone? You'd better not say that in front of Lucille."

"She's been doing a terrific job."

"That's what I was afraid of."

"Oh, you." He grabbed me and pulled me into his lap. "Do you think I could possibly do any of this without you. Where the *hell* have you been?"

I pulled myself off his lap, hoping no one had seen that. "It sounds like you missed me."

"Oh? Were you gone? I really love your hair. Have you turned into a Parisian girly girl?"

I gave him a look.

"Just checking," he said.

"Look, I wrote you that Scott's ship with the other musicians will be getting in in a few days. You're going to be at the dock to meet him, aren't you?"

"Oh. Uh, sure. Uh, yeah. Give me the time again."

"Wednesday, three. He was pretty upset, you know, that you didn't write to him very often while he was away."

"I was busy running *two* clubs. And, well . . . writing letters, it's not something well, you know I . . . How many did *you* get from me?"

"None."

"See?"

Marty jumped down from the stage and we were quickly in each other's arms.

"You in a tux and a bow tie? I'm shocked."

Max went back to fixing things that didn't need fixing.

"Well, you know," Marty said. "Have to play the game sometimes."

I was used to seeing Marty in his sloppy corduroy pants, his jacket with the patches on the elbow, and his tie poking out of his jacket pocket.

"And that tan? How'd you find the time?"

"Hollywood is the land of tans. Not having one is practically a sin. Oh gosh, Al, it's good to see you." He brought me back into his arms and squeezed me. "The way we left off . . . Before you went to Paris . . . I was in bad shape, and the ungrateful letters I sent you . . ."

"Forget it. I just felt bad that the only part I had for you was the Easter Bunny at kids' backyard parties, but you did meet a couple of producers."

"Yes, I did. I would never do anything to hurt you. You know that, don't you? I mean, if I ever did anything to hurt *you,* I'd want to bump myself off."

"*Please*. I already have one friend I have to worry about keeping alive. I don't want two."

"Who?"

"Scott. Remember me running back and forth to the hospital before Paris because he—"

"Oh yeah, right. I'd never really do that. It's just an expression. How *is* Scott? Where is he?"

"He'll be home Wednesday. He's taking the ship back from Paris so he can keep track of the musical instruments and the musicians."

"I don't know him very well, but he seems like a good guy, and I'd never want to hurt him either. You know that. Don't you? Never. Really, Al, I wouldn't want to—"

"Of course not. I'd never expect you to. Why are you going on like that?"

"No reason." He looked down at his shoes like a kid. "It's just I want you to know . . . Well, I know I owe my success to you, so I'd never want to hurt you or anyone you care about. I mean, if it hadn't been for you getting me that part in *All's Well that Doesn't End*, I'd still be in East Hampton in a bunny costume."

"Tell me. Was that show as bad as it sounds?"

"A musical Shakespearean western? What do you think?"

We both laughed.

"*But*, it got me noticed by Columbia and it got me that seven-year contract so I'm—"

Everything stopped. Silence. Everyone turned to stare. Even the diners stopped their dinner conversations to turn and look. Juliana had just entered the room. She wore a royal blue silk gown that caressed her breasts and midriff and opened into layers of cloth bouncing around her hidden legs down to the floor. It was held up with spaghetti straps. She'd covered her naked décolletage with a single silver strand that held a teardrop diamond pointing toward her upraised breasts. A pair of cluster diamond earrings sat on her ear lobes. Her arms were covered with royal blue gloves extending from her fingertips to her elbows. Watching her glide toward us, I could barely catch my breath. Richard, in a tux, walked by her side, his arm linked in hers, but it took a few minutes before I noticed *him*.

Lucille threw her arms around Juliana like they were old buddies, when I knew they had only met once. Not being given to public displays of affection, especially superficial ones (probably learned from her father's side of the family), Juliana gave her a quick squeeze and removed herself from Lucille's grasp. She moved past me without even a nod—ouch—and extended her gloved hand to Max. He took it and kissed her on the cheek, "You look lovely, my dear. Richard, may I steal your wife for a moment? I want to show her around the place."

"Oh, sure," Richard said, handing his wife over to Max. "Be my guest."

"I will," Max said as he wrapped Juliana's gloved arm around his. They walked off.

"Murder!" Lucille exclaimed, slapping her two gloved hands together as she watched Juliana go. "That package is solid."

Richard whispered to me, "What'd she say?"

"Roughly translated, Lucille thinks Juliana is perfection."

"Oh. She is, she is," Richard said. "Thank you, Lucille."

Lucille winked at him and patted my shoulder. "You keep cool, hon. I'm taking it tonight. Back in a tick." She scurried off to her office, her dress swishing loudly as she went.

A new singer, an attractive young man, stood at the mike singing "Stardust." It brought back memories of World War II and my first flashes of excitement at just being in the same room with Juliana. Oh, how I wished I could go up on that stage and cut in.

"That's my cue to go backstage," Marty said. "I have to rest the pipes. I'm opening for Vic Damone tonight. Hey! That's another thing I owe you. Tonight."

"Not me. I didn't set it up."

"No, Lucille did."

"Lucille?"

"Yeah. But I'm sure if I weren't your client *and* your friend, she never would've gone out on that limb for me. You're good for me, Al. Glad you're home."

He kissed me on the cheek and ran off. Lucille had set up this gig for him? Not Max? Could that be why she betrayed me? To get my job? I thought back to the time when I first met Lucille. She'd played the accompaniment for that girl who did the striptease for me and could have trapped me into one helluva moral mess. Then later she came begging for a job as a secretary, claiming she had no idea what that girl was going to do. And I fell for that. And I hired her! She was plotting back then to get my job. How could I have been so stupid! It was Lucille. Lucille betrayed us with Schuyler. But how did Lucille know about Juliana and me? She was always hanging around. Working more than she should. Probably snooping. It had to be her.

More couples stepped onto the dance floor, among them Mr. and Mrs. Al Miniaci, who owned Paramount Automat. We had to buy our coin-ops from them. Both were always elegantly dressed in the finest quality clothes. In '51, Al's wife, Rose, got polio, that horrible disease that used to cripple and kill children and adults by the thousands. They finally got a vaccination for it last year. Doctors said Mrs. Miniaci would never walk again. But Mr. Miniaci loved her so much he wouldn't stop till he found a cure. He finally found it in Hot Springs, Arkansas, so now she only had a little bit of a limp and the two of them looked real good on the dance floor. Mr. Miniaci never brought a girl to the club like the others did. I'd heard he stayed pretty faithful to the missus.

Jimmy, "the Crusher," came in with a new side kick, a skinny kid in a suit and tie that was too big for him. His dark hair flopped over his forehead and into his eyes. The two of them moved toward their ring-side seats. Neither had brought a date. Jimmy always came alone. Not many girls would want to be seen with a man who had half a melted face, a deep scar across his forehead, and a right hand with no thumb. Jimmy wasn't easy to look at, but you got used to it. Sort of. A few more tough mob guys with girls on their arms gathered around ringside with Jimmy.

Frank Costello entered the dining room with a woman on his arm and lit a cigarette.

Boy, was he in a peck of trouble. Taxes. Not paying them. Or so the government said. They still hadn't quite proven it yet, but they were getting pretty close.

"Hey, Al," he said, coming toward me. "Back from Paris, huh? Good trip?"

"Yeah, very good, Mr. Costello."

"Hey, what's that mister bit, like ya don't hardly know me? I'm yer Uncle Frank."

"Okay. Uncle Frank."

"Datta-goil. Oh, and this here's the missus. I don't think yer ever met Missus Costello."

"No. I haven't. Pleased to meet you, Mrs. Costello."

She nodded without speaking.

Frank never brought women to the club with him, his wife or otherwise. The other guys, except for Mr. Miniaci, brought their Friday night ladies, even if it was Saturday.

"Ya know, Lauretta, Al—Alice, she's just the sort you gotta know. *She's* got class. *She's* got a college education. Maybe you could show her 'round town sometime, Al—Alice. My wife'd prob'ly like calling you Alice better. More girlie. So, what do you think about maybe showing my wife round town. Introduce her to the celebrity folk you know. None of the sleezeballs. Oh, but you prob'ly don't know those types, a nice goil like yourself." He turned to his wife. "You'd like that, Lauretta, going round town with Alice. Wouldn't ya?"

She nodded with that shy smile again.

So, what ya say, Alice?"

I really hated him calling me Alice, but how do you tell that to the Prime Minister of the Underworld. "Uh, well, uh, sure. Sometime."

"Yer a good egg, Alice. See, hon?" Frank said, turning back to his wife. "Alice knows some real decent folk. That's who ya oughta be meetin'. Thanks, Alice. Oh, we need a table for just us. I don't want Lauretta sittin' with them clowns over there. Ya know what I mean?"

"Sure, Mr.—"

"What?"

"Uncle Frank."

"Datta goil."

I signaled to the maître 'd and told him to escort the Costellos to a table for two down front.

"Thanks, Al," 'Uncle Frank' said as he swatted me on the rear. He guided Lauretta toward the table, following the maître d'. I suppose I should've introduced Richard to him. He was standing right next to me, but I wasn't sure how to introduce Richard to someone like "Uncle Frank."

The gangly kid who came in with Jimmy the Crusher hurried toward me, calling, "Hey!" He pushed Richard out of the way.

"Excuse me?" Richard said, indignant

"Yeah, yer excused, old man." Then turning to me. "You Al Huffman?"

"Yes."

"Well, I'm Sammy and I got somefin' fer ya." He reached into his pants pocket and I backed up, my heart thundering. A gun? He drew out a folded paper square and held it out for me. "It's from my buddy, Jimmy, over dere." I took it from his sweaty fingers that appeared not to have been washed in some time and started breathing again. I sure must've been away a long time if these guys could unglue me on my own turf.

Sammy ran back to the table with Jimmy and the other boys. Mr. and Mrs. Miniaci were just taking their own seats around the table.

"My goodness," Richard said. "Who in the world was that? Certainly an unsavory type. Shouldn't you take that note to the police?"

"The police? Uh . . . no. Everything's fine." Richard didn't know we never called the police. Ever. Not if we wanted to stay in business. They stopped by to pick up their take once a week, but we never *called* them. There was so much we didn't tell Richard.

I opened the square of paper. Inside, in an unsteady hand, was written:

"Well cum hom
I mist yu"

"Well?" Richard said. "I don't mean to pry, but could you be in danger?"

"No. It's nothing." I refolded the square and placed it in the waist-band of my dress. I could feel Jimmy watching me from his ringside seat. I recalled that bracelet he'd given me for my thirtieth birth-day/graduation two years ago. I wasn't sure what . . . I didn't want to think about what this meant. I gave Jimmy a quick wave, but no smile.

"Well, Richard. Everyone seems to be off dancing. Shall we sit? Order a drink?"

"I don't think you and I have ever danced together," he said. "How about it?"

"I don't know. You're used to dancing with Juliana."

"Not in a long time. She's always busy dancing with everybody else. Business." He took my hand. "Let's go."

The singer had begun "The Way You Look Tonight." Richard put his arm across my back and led me in a very pleasant fox trot. "You know, Richard, it's kind of funny that after all the years we've spent together in clubs waiting for Juliana, we never once thought to dance with each other. Isn't that strange?"

"I think we were always so worried about Juliana we couldn't relax long enough to even have the thought. But I feel like this play is going to be good for her. There isn't going be much to worry about anymore."

My stomach flip-flopped.

"You dance very well," he said.

"I don't believe you, but I appreciate your kindness. How's your mother?"

"Oh, Al," he sighed. "Mothers. You must have had one too."

I laughed. "Oh, I did. A humdinger of a one. Tell me about yours."

"I'm sure she'd give *your* mother a run for her money. My mother's a very nervous woman. She always has been, since I was a child. She doesn't much care for my older sister, so when she gets her bouts of frozen anxiety syndrome I have to leave in a moment's notice."

"Frozen anxiety syndrome? What's that?"

"It's anything that makes it impossible for my mother to get out of bed and take care of herself. It can go on for weeks or even months. And she won't let anyone but me take care of her."

"That's why you have to dash off all the time."

"Exactly. But this last time, just before I was to leave for Paris, she actually had a real honest-to-goodness heart attack. That scared the life out of my sister and me. I mean, for Mother to actually have some-thing real and that serious. We never expected it. I was so grateful that you could go to Paris in my stead and be with Juliana. I know what a great imposition that must've been on your own life."

"Oh, well, it, uh . . . Not very much."

"You're just being kind. You know, Al, I love my mother, but my goodness she's a lot of work. And she's not very nice to Juliana. She doesn't like me being married to a singer. She wishes I married a traditional girl and had children . . ." I thought I detected sadness in his voice when he said children. "But I'm sure that's what all mothers want for their sons. She doesn't understand what a special girl Juliana is. Mother calls Juliana a dance hall girl. To her face. But to me she calls her a prostitute. I never expect Julie to visit her. Why should she put up with that? Oh, but you don't want to hear this. Especially not while we're dancing."

A few more couples had joined us on the dance floor. I glanced at Juliana and Max dancing. They looked perfectly suited to each other. I wondered what they had to say after all the years that had gone by. I thought maybe while they were dancing, Max would tell her his plan for getting her out of Schuyler's contract. Did he have such a plan? He didn't when we were in Paris.

"No. Richard, I like listening to you. Reminds me of my own crazy mother. I wonder if she's still alive."

"What?"

"I haven't seen my mother in fourteen years."

"Why?"

"Oh . . ." I felt close to him and I wanted to tell him about that last time I spoke to Mom. We were on the phone and she yelled "queer" at me. It was right after my wedding when my fiancé walked in and caught Juliana and I kissing. Of course, that meant the wedding was off. And of course, I couldn't share this story with Richard. "No real reason we haven't seen each other," I said. "Things that just happen between people. You know."

"Mothers aren't easy, are they?"

I laughed. "If only you knew mine."

"Tell me. Let's go sit at the table and you tell me. We'll swap mother stories."

When I turned to step off the dance floor, my innards froze like Richard's mother. The tables were only half full and it was already past ten on a Saturday night. It should be jammed by now with customers in

formal wear clamoring for their waiters. A few waiters stood at attention
at their stations, waiting for someone to serve. Richard guided me to a
large round table where we would all gather soon for dinner and the
show. He helped me into a chair, which was actually needed because of all
the silk and lace gathered around my waist and legs cascading in a flare
down toward the floor. "Do you want something to eat?" Richard asked.

"No, I'll wait for the others, but I'd love a drink."

"A sidecar like my wife. Right?"

"Yes. No! I'll have a Manhattan."

Richard lit a Marlboro and gave our drink order to the waiter. He
leaned toward me. "So, tell me about your mother. I'm betting she
can't outdo mine for being a pain in the, the . . . neck."

I laughed, knowing what word he really wanted to use. "Well," I
began, "my mother used to hear voices that told her I was a demon
trying to kill her."

His brow wrinkled. "I think you're going to win."

"She chased me around the house with a kitchen knife once. She
didn't mean it. She thought she was protecting herself from a
demon. Me."

"You're a lot more generous than I would be. What'd you do?"

"Ran. My father tackled her to the ground and grabbed the knife
away. It only happened once."

"Only!"

"It left an impression, though."

"I would think so."

"I think the worst was when she locked me out of the house for the
whole night. That happened a lot."

"How old were you?"

The orchestra singer was singing "What is This Thing Called
Love?"

"It happened off and on from age eight to twelve. When my father
was working the all-night shift in a bakery, I'd sleep under the porch,
and when he came home he'd find me there and know that Mom had
had another one of her spells. He'd feel bad and take me to Finnegan's,
this diner where my grandma was a waitress. Grandma wasn't there in

the early morning, so Dad and I could get away with having strawberry
ice cream for breakfast."

The waiter placed our drinks in front of us and we each took a sip.

"Didn't your father do anything to stop this?"

"What could he do? He had to work. Our neighbors were terrified
of her. Sometimes Mrs. Boyd from next door would find me under the
porch and take me into her house. I liked Mrs. Boyd. Her son, Danny,
was my beau throughout my childhood. We came to New York
together."

"Where's Danny now?"

"I'm not sure. I read a few years ago that he was getting married to
a girl from our town, but I don't know where they settled."

"He should've married *you*."

My mind flashed back to the time when I found Danny naked in
Max's apartment. "I don't think that would've worked out."

Richard lit another Marlboro and shook his head. "You'd make
someone a terrific wife," he said seriously. "But you don't want to get
married, do you?"

"Not really."

"I've never met a girl like you. So, in charge, so confident. I guess I
should stop introducing you to those Omaha businessmen, hmm?"

"I think so. I never dreamt of marriage as a child like I've heard
other girls do. When I was eight, I decided I was going to do something completely, absolutely wonderful, but I didn't know what that
something was."

"But having children wasn't it?"

"No. Do you think I'm awful?"

"Not after what you've done for Juliana. Is helping Juliana the
completely, absolutely wonderful something you wanted to do?"

"I don't know. I've never really asked myself that, but . . ." Tears
filled my eyes. I tried hard not to let them fall, but they did anyway. I
felt like I was losing everything I'd ever worked for, that my whole life
was about to end.

"What's the matter?"

"Nothing." I rummaged through my purse. "Where is that handkerchief?"

"Here take mine." He took his from his inside pocket.

I blotted my eyes. "I have no idea why, I'm getting so uh . . ."

"Perhaps it's because Juliana is about to have one of the greatest successes of her career and it's all because of you and that eight-year-old girl who dreamt of doing a completely, absolutely wonderful something."

We smiled at each other, not sure how to move on from this moment that was warm, but awkward too. "Well . . ." I said, averting my eyes from his. "Look, Juliana's still dancing with Max."

The young singer was singing "Begin the Beguine." A circle had formed around Juliana and Max. No one could not watch them; they had become one dancer. Diners sitting behind their tables slowly rose to get a better view. Max and Juliana had no awareness of being scrutinized. They were lost in the music and in the perfect movement of their bodies completely in tune with each other. It was like they knew exactly what the other would do through some supernatural means. The two of them invented moves right on the spot, neither getting lost. They were simply having fun, oblivious to what surrounded them; it was the kind of fun they might have had when they were both new to each other. My heart pounded with longing watching Juliana's heels move in perfect time to every move Max made, never missing a beat. I heard a few whispered "oohs" and "aahs" coming from the audience when Max swung her out and twirled her back into his chest. She was sensuous as she moved her hips, walking toward him. Their bodies pressed together and then out again. At the end, Max bent Juliana over in the most graceful dip I'd ever seen. As they remained in the pose, gazing into each other's eyes, they seemed like a work of art created by a long-ago master. My hormones raged within me. It took all my power to stop me from running up on stage and grabbing her. I looked to my right and saw Richard's eyes riveted on Juliana. I thought he and I might be having the same the struggle. I didn't like having *that* in common with him. When Max rose from the dip, bringing Juliana close to him, the whole audience applauded. Max and Juliana looked genuinely surprised that anyone had been watching them. They held hands, laughing, as they made a silly bow.

The singer began again with "Cheek to Cheek." Max encouraged everyone to dance and stop staring at Juliana and him. He and Juliana danced to this faster tune.

"I've never met Max's wife," Richard said. "Do you know her?"

"Max isn't married."

He turned back toward the stage. "Really? I knew he wasn't long ago when I first met him, but surely I thought by now . . . A handsome, successful—"

"Never found the right woman," I hurried to say.

"Oh. Shall we join them?"

"Who?"

"Juliana and Max. Up there."

"Oh, yes, of course. Let's."

As we moved toward the dance floor, Giorgio, the doorman, came running in, his gray ringlets bouncing. "Missa Al, here. For you." He pushed an envelope into my hand. "I go quick. Watcha dah door." Giorgio was a good guy. We never caught him in some corner grabbing a smoke. We could depend on him to be standing proud at our door, no matter what the weather. He'd been with us since the beginning.

"What is it," Richard asked. "A welcome home card?"

"I have no idea."

I opened the envelope and slid out a card with a cartoon of a duck in a French beret on the front. The duck was painting a picture of the Eiffel tower on his easel. Across the top in script it read, "You inspire me." Jimmy again? No, he couldn't write like that.

"That's a funny thing to get. Open it and see who sent it."

I was about to flip open the card and see what the joke was when suddenly—I knew who sent it and my blood went cold. I shoved it back into the envelope as I looked up to see Juliana and Max dancing. "Uh, Richard, I don't mean to be rude, but I just remembered who might've sent it. An old friend. And I think I should read it—"

"Oh, of course. You want to read it alone. How thoughtless of me. Go ahead I'll just . . ." His eyes were focused on Max and Juliana.

I ran toward my office but stopped when I saw Bart. He was dressed in his white tuxedo, jaunting over to the ringside table. "Hey, Al," he threw at me, waving as he passed by. I turned to see him hand-shaking and backslapping the mob guys. I knew Bart was a lowlife, but

I'd never connected him with those types. Then, I remember that threat he sang to me the day I fired him. "There'll come a time when you'll regret it." I hurried off to my office, snapped on the light, and closed the door.

Standing at my desk, the card shaking in my hand, I took a few deep breaths. I pulled the card from its envelope and opened it. On the inside, written in block print, it read, "Welcome home. See the gift I left on your desk." I was not surprised by the signature. "Best Regards, Dan Schuyler." Gift? What gift? I didn't see anything on my desk. Just the blotter, the dictograph, and my rock paperweight. I lifted the paperweight. There sat a page that had been torn from a book. In the center of the page was a paragraph that had been circled in black ink.

"Some lesbians manifest pronounced sadistic and psychopathic trends."

I opened the bottom drawer of my desk and took out the book, *Female Homosexuality*. That was the book one of Schuyler's stooges had left on my desk before I went to Paris. I thumbed through it to see if any pages had been torn out. Toward the end of the book, I saw that page 302 was gone. There was no number on the page I held in my hand, but it lined up with the scraggly edges of the missing 302 perfectly. My heart pounded. He'd been in my office. How had he gotten in while I was only a few feet away talking to Richard? I peered under my desk, threw open the closet door. No Schuyler. How silly. He'd never be so obvious. Maybe it had been one my betrayers! Yes, of course. All three suspects were right outside the door. Was it Bertha? No, Lucille? No! No, it was Bart. He was the type who would make friends with a man like that.

I threw the book back in the drawer and walked out of the office. I was careful to lock the door, but that was pretty much like locking up the proverbial horse after . . . well, you know. I hurried over to Richard, who was standing in the back, watching Max and Juliana still dancing. My eyes roamed the room, foolishly looking for Schuyler.

"Everything all right?" he asked me.

"Fine."

"Max sure is dancing a lot with Juliana."

"Al, it's a mess. A complete mess," Juliana said into the other end of the phone. She was sitting in a phone booth in a drug store in Philly. "How could you have gotten me into something like this?"

My breath temporarily shot away from me and I couldn't respond. Finally, I said—slowly—deliberately, "*I* didn't get you into this. Dan Schuyler did."

"Of course. I'm just so rattled . . ."

"At least, I didn't mean to. I still haven't figured out which one of my so-called colleagues betrayed—"

"Oh, it doesn't matter who. It's done."

"It matters to me. Hold on a sec." I pushed a button on my dictograph. "Lucille."

"Jackson!" she squawked at me.

"Hold all my calls till I tell you different."

"Solid!" she said.

I really had to have a talk with Lucille. Then a thought . . . Could her sudden jive talk be a reason for firing her? I went back to the phone. "Jule, I'm back." I slipped the earring off my phone ear, so I could hear her better.

"It's the play," she said. "What they're doing to it. They yanked out three songs yesterday and put in two new ones. We open tomorrow night!"

"That's how tryouts are. Lots of changes at the last minute. You've had to deal with that in the clubs too."

"Never like this. No one seems to know what they're doing. One of the songs they cut was perfect for my voice. And they still haven't found a real choreographer yet. They've got this kid ballet dancer flying around the stage, and I think he's supposed to be choreo-graphing—"

"Paulie Nelson."

"Yes. That's him."

"He's Harry Fielding's nephew."

"*Our* Harry Fielding, the director?"

"Of course. Who else?"

"Well, *our* Harry Fielding doesn't seem to trust him."

"He doesn't."

"Oh, terrific."

"The scuttlebutt around Broadway is when Harry said yes to directing *Heaven,* he promised his sister he'd give the kid a shot. Harry's got a good rep around town though, so I don't think he'll—"

"He's trying to make up for the kid by directing the acting *and* the dancing. Only he doesn't know the first thing about being graceful. He's got us all clomping around the stage like drunken circus elephants."

I slapped my hand to my mouth so she couldn't hear me laughing.

"Schuyler's a nervous wreck," she continued, "and keeps pacing in the back of the rehearsal studio. Why doesn't he *do* something besides threaten me?"

"Has he said anything to you about—you know, in front of other people?"

"No. He wouldn't. Almost everyone in the cast belongs to *our* 'club.' He'd be outnumbered."

"Maybe that's it. Tell the others in the cast what he's doing and—"

"And what? They'll defend me against him? I tell them this and you won't find one single, you know, in the bunch. Except for me, of course, who just committed professional suicide. Al, the stress is soft-ening your brain."

"Of course, you're right. I don't know what I was thinking. It all just makes me so damn mad. I want to punch someone."

"What's unnerving *me* is that Schuyler isn't out hiring a choreogra-pher and a new musical director. He's supposed to be the producer. When is he going to produce?"

"I wonder if he's running out of money?"

"What? With only half a show? Have you heard anything. I'm in a disaster, aren't I?"

"No, no. Harry'll pull it together." How could I have said such a thing to her?

"Yesterday, Schuyler dressed down the juvenile in the cruelest language. This morning the poor kid looked shell-shocked and couldn't get a note out. And poor book writer, Josh. A delightful boy. This book he's written is a lot better than the last horror he wrote for me. It's a really good book. Even *you* said so. But Schuyler, and Harry too, keep telling him to make these ridiculous changes and the kid won't stand up to them. They're ruining his script. I won't be able to take another" —she whispered— "flop. And if I do . . . flop," she choked out, "*then* what will Schuyler do to me?"

"Well, that might be a way out of this."

"Don't even joke about a thing like that. I fail and Schuyler throws me in the ashcan of life? Then I can go back to abject obscurity where no one gives a darn what I do in the bedroom?"

"I always care what you do in the bedroom."

"Al! What if someone heard you?"

"Oh. I forgot." My heartbeat sped up. "The door's closed. No one can hear through that."

"You're sure?"

Through the window in my door, I saw Bertha walk by. "I think."

"You think?"

"No. I *know*. No one can hear through that door."

"You've got to be careful."

"I know. I know. Just concentrate on doing your best. Think about those Copa reviews you got last month. Just think about your voice and—"

"Can you come here?"

"You want me to?" I could practically feel her hand reaching out for me through the phone wires. She never did that before. Never so boldly open, but . . . "Schuyler?"

"As my manager."

"He knows I'm not."

She was quiet for a few moments and I waited, listening to her breath, wishing I could touch her. Finally, she said, "They're predicting a blizzard for tomorrow. Three, four inches of snow. Maybe no one will show up."

"You're gonna be good, Jule. No. Great. You're going to be great. I know it. I *feel* it. Get them to put a phone in your dressing room. When the coast is clear, call me here at my office before you go on tomorrow night."

I put the phone back in its cradle just as my hand began to shake. Had I reset the privacy button after I spoke to Lucille? I was afraid to look, but . . . It was still open. Heart pounding. Did Lucille listen in?

We couldn't go on like this. The strain of being caught, saying the wrong thing, doing the wrong thing . . . It was too much. Exhausting. I stood outside my office. The door to Max's office was partially ajar and I could see him in there working. I hadn't seen him in the Haven office for quite some time, a couple years. Since the beginning when we first opened the Haven, he'd left it pretty much up to me to run. I wondered if he knew just how much stress this show was putting on Juliana; it could ruin her performance. Maybe I should tell him. He could come up with a plan to get her out of the show, away from Schuyler.

I walked over to his office, poked my head in, and knocked on the open door. "May I?'

Max nodded, not looking up from his work.

"Max?" I said to the top of his head. He continued to pour over the papers on his desk, his white shirt open at the neck, his sleeves rolled up. I'd never seen him at the club when he didn't wear a jacket and a tie. Even during the day. An open briefcase lay on the desk near the telephone. He scribbled something on a pad of paper.

"Yeah? What is it?" he asked, impatient, still not looking up.

"I'm, well, worried."

"So am I."

"Not too much, I hope. You're the one I'm counting on. You know. To take care of—"

"Have you seen—?"

"The play isn't going well in Philadelphia. What happens if it flops out of town and never makes it to New York? What happens to Jule? You are working on a plan to get her out of that?"

"I can't think about that now." He ran a hand roughly through his almost-all-gray hair. "Have you seen this?"

"But you have to think about it now. If that play nosedives . . ."

"Have you seen these goddamn numbers, Al?" He shouted, banging a fist onto the papers. "Have you been watching them like you're supposed to?"

"I've been in Paris for four months!" I shouted back. "I've been back barely a month."

"A month is enough time for you to see we're in trouble. Our audiences at the Haven have been steadily dwindling. Why haven't you told me?"

"I'm taking care of it."

"How? By watching us lose money every week? We can't sustain this."

"I'll fix it. I've been busy trying to figure out who betrayed me and how to keep Schuyler away and—"

"Too busy to do your job?"

"I *always* do my job!"

"I've got to get to the Mt. Olympus." He got up, pulling his suit jacket over his wrinkled shirt. "Call Shirl and tell her to meet me there."

"Oh, you mean like I'm your secretary?"

"If you act like a secretary, you'll be treated like one. If you want something better, start by forgetting that nonsense with Schuyler—"

"Nonsense?"

"Or you and I both'll end up on the double trouble bread line." He gathered his papers and threw them into the open briefcase. "And would you *please* talk to Virginia. I don't know what's wrong with her, but she's chosen the absolute worst time in my life to go crazy. *Do* something. I must be paying you for *some* reason." He pulled his overcoat onto his right shoulder and charged out of his office.

CHAPTER 4

*S*he slammed the door.

Oh, God, what a day. "Virginia, open this please."

"No!" she yelled back through the bronze letter slot. "Go away."

"I can't."

I had no time for this. And yet there I stood on Virginia's porch, next to her flowerpot with the dead flowers flopping over the side. The Virginia I knew would never have allowed her flowers to die that way. I thought of the African violets she had moved into Max's MacDougal Street apartment when she took it over during the war. Back then, she told me that African violets must always be watered from the bottom, never the top. Flowers were important to Virginia. She had filled Max's apartment with cut flowers that she'd had delivered every other day by the florist down the block. Her mother had not permitted flowers in their home because she said they were a waste of money. Virginia used to hide her African violets in her bedroom when she still lived in the uptown mansion, but now her mother was gone. So why were those flowers dead?

I'd never been to Virginia's East 64th Street townhouse near Second Avenue, and it hadn't been such an easy job getting there. The snowbanks made the roads hard for the bus to get around, and the construction along Park Avenue and Fifty-Seventh had slowed the traffic to a crawl. I had so much to do back at the club I could barely sit still in my seat. I wanted to go out and show that cop how to direct traffic. Lately, the city was always tearing something down, putting something up. Now they were taking down the Park Avenue apartments and putting up huge office buildings. One of them was gonna be fifty stories tall! Max had helped Virginia sell her mansion a few years back when the city was tearing those down and putting up modern apartment buildings or turning them into fancy museums. It was darn annoying, all these changes. But Virginia got a nice price and was able to give some money to her old English butler, Ainsworth, who left the US to retire in England, and her old Irish maid, Nola, who'd been waiting on Virginia since Virginia was a little girl. I didn't know who was attending to Virginia's needs now, but I couldn't picture her living alone with no help.

"Virginia!" I called to her through the mail slot again. "Max's worried about you."

"No, he's not," came her response back from the mail slot.

"He is and so am I."

"Hah!"

I'd telephoned Virginia before I came, but she hung up.

"Virginia, come on! It's freezing out here." I kicked up some leftover snow that lay in a clump on the porch near the wrought iron railing. I should've worn galoshes instead of these stupid heels. "Virginia!"

"You don't like me anymore," came through the letter slot. "You think I'm a bad woman."

"No, I don't."

Did I? Of course not. Then why hadn't I seen her since Christmas, three years ago, when Scott was in the hospital and his grandma, Mattie, was staying with Max and me. I saw her with Max a few times after that, but we never had a lot to say to each other anymore. Something had changed between us after that awful thing Moose did to her. I didn't seem able to look at her; it was like *she* was the one who'd done something wrong, instead of Moose. But I *knew* it was him, not her. It was Moose who had made her. . . put his thing in her mouth. I mean what could she do? He had a gun at her head. If Jimmy the Crusher hadn't come in and chopped Moose's hand off . . . Oh gosh, I hated thinking about that. Blood everywhere. My stomach felt sick with the memory. Blood, semen, and later toothpaste all over Virginia's face . . . I couldn't keep those pictures out of my head, and whenever I got near her, that's all I saw. She didn't seem to like being with me anymore either. She always looked down at the ground or far off in the distance, like she wasn't in the same room with me. I could hardly remember how she and I used to be before. I had vague memories of having lunch with her at Schrafft's. And those cloudy memories made a good feeling come over me and, for a little while, I remembered our friendship. Why couldn't we just forget those few minutes in that room in the club and go back to being how we used to be? We'd known each other for years, since before the war. What were a few moments compared to that? Why should those memories take over everything?

I slammed my hand against the doorbell. It made a pleasant chiming sound, and I was in no mood for a pleasant sound. "Virginia, darn-it! Just let me in for a minute to warm up. Then I'll go."

I waited, my hands stuffed deep in the pockets of my full-length chinchilla coat. As I paced, the cold air made my face hurt. *And* I was getting a headache. I had to get back to the office and work on our slow ticket sales problem and find a way to keep Juliana calm and build her confidence.

What's wrong with Max? I wondered as I shoved my hands into my armpits, trying to warm them. I'd dashed out of my office so fast I forgot my gloves. Darn, Max was the one with contacts. The kind that make people pay attention. Why wasn't he doing anything? *He* could get Schuyler and Harry a good crew, one that would make Juliana safe. He could get Schuyler to stop threatening her. So why wasn't he? If he didn't do something and soon, I would . . . What? What could *I* do? The secret investor! Yes! That's it! Appeal to the secret investor. I stomped my feet to get feeling back. I had to find him first. He was, after all, secret, but there must be some . . . Shirl! Of course. She was in the money part of the business. Maybe *she* knew him. And if the guy was in love with Juliana, he wouldn't want her to be hurt, so that meant . . . He was straight. My heart sunk down to my stomach. I couldn't tell him about this.

"Virginia! Open this door, darn-it! I can't stay on this porch freezing my rear end off all day. If you don't open this door, I'm going to . . . You used to be such a kind person."

The door inched opened a sliver. I could see one of Virginia's eyes squinting at me. "You used to be kind too," she said.

Before she could shut the door again, I pushed both hands against it with all my weight, which admittedly wasn't much. If my quick calculations were correct, my thirty-two-year-old strength should easily hold out against her forty-nine-year-old muscles. I continued to push with everything I had, but the door wouldn't budge. *My gosh, what does this woman eat?* There really must be something to that Wheaties thing!

"Go away. You don't care about me," she yelled, and didn't even appear to be winded. I took in a deep breath and pushed as hard as I could; the door and Virginia moved back slightly. But it was enough for me to squeeze my slight body through. Inside, I gulped at the air, trying to catch my breath. Then I saw why it'd been so hard for me. Virginia had wedged a heavy wooden chair against the door.

She ran into the next room, screaming, "Don't come in! Don't come in!"

I ran after her and found her in the middle of a large room, standing ankle deep in crumpled newspapers, half-eaten spaghetti on unwashed china plates, orange peels, uneaten, rotting TV dinners, open books in ragged, cascading piles, china cups, some broken, some filled with brown gunk that might have been coffee at one time, a few broken wine bottles, a jelly jar with the jelly smeared around the floor, smashed tomatoes, and other unrecognizable eatables and uneatables.

Ants and roaches crawled in and out of the boxes and through the wine bottles, the jelly jar, and a rotten cucumber. There wasn't one surface where some crawly thing didn't crawl. It made me itchy. Virginia's hair was a knotted, uncombed mess and it looked like she hadn't washed it in some time. Her cotton flower-print dress was torn and dirty. It hung on her like an old rag; she'd lost a lot of weight. "So now you know!" she shouted. "Go! Go! Go!" She slowly sunk to her knees in tears into the center of the refuse pile.

I stood stuck to my spot, so ashamed. "Virginia, I'm—I'm sorry," I said. "So sorry I haven't been here to help you. I want to help you now.

We're going to get this place cleaned up and you cleaned up and get you some type of help. Oh gosh, Virginia, I'm so sorry."

I walked back into the foyer, stepping around roaches scurrying past my feet, hoping not to run into a rat. I found the phone on the floor and dialed. "Lucille, is Max there?"

"No!" Virginia screamed, running to me. She yanked the phone out of my hand and hung it up. "Please, you can't. I beg you." She started to fold onto her knees.

"Oh geez, Virginia, don't do that." I held her up by the elbows, preventing her from collapsing at my feet. "Think. Think," I said out loud to myself, then turned to Virginia. "Okay. Look, here's what we're gonna do. I'll help you get washed and I'll get you a good meal. We'll get your hair done. Then, we'll call Max and—"

"No!"

"Virginia, Max knows something's up. I don't know what he knows because he didn't tell me, but he sent me to see you. He's worried. Have you been in touch with him?"

She held her hands near her mouth as if ashamed of what she said to Max. "I call him. Sometimes." She whimpered like a frightened child. "I only want to hear his voice on the phone. I don't want to bother him. I don't want him to come here. Heavens, no. I just call him, but he has all those men . . ."

"All those men? Not anymore. He only has one. Scott."

"Oh!" She backed away from me. "I wasn't supposed to tell. Don't tell him I told. Please don't tell him."

"Look, Virginia—" I said slowly, trying to think and having trouble.

"No. Don't tell him."

"I can't handle all of this at once. The first thing—the first thing we have to do is, uh, uh, make you well. That's what we have to do. But first we—we have to get you cleaned up. Then—then—then we have to, to, uh, uh . . ."

"Don't leave me alone. Please, Al."

"No. We never should've left you alone in the first place."

"You think I'm a bad woman, don't you?"

"No. Of course, not." Oh, how I wanted that to be true. "Come here." I reached out for her and pulled her into my arms, despite the smell. I flicked off the roach that was crawling up her back.

———

I managed to clean up Virginia in her upstairs bathroom. Amazingly, the whole upper floor was fine; a little dusty, but no garbage. Her bed was made and looked as if it had never been slept in. Even the bathroom seemed fine. She must've been living mostly in that one room.

While she was drying herself off, I scurried down the stairs to the foyer to call Max. I didn't like leaving her alone up there, but I needed to get Max involved. All during the bath she chatted with me like it was old times, like we were having lunch at Schrafft's.

Max didn't answer his two office phones or his home phone. I just stood there in the foyer, shaking. *I can't do all this alone.* The club's in trouble, Virginia's in trouble, Juliana's in trouble: the club, Virginia, Jule. My breathing sped up with the chaotic rhythm of my thoughts. I was on the verge of panic. *No, Al! You can't do that. You don't have time for that.* Slow down. Calm. Breathe like Juliana on opening night. I took a deep breath in and let it float out of me. It's all gonna be okay. Easy. Take it easy. Yes, easy.

I ran back upstairs to Virginia. She stood in front of the bathroom mirror tying the big bow to her silk blouse. The skirt she chose was a swirl of colors. I thought that must be a good sign. She almost looked like her old self, except her brown hair, damp from being washed, clung to her neck and shoulders. I didn't think I'd ever seen her with her hair down. Hmm, letting her hair down. That wasn't something that had ever been very easy for Virginia; now she'd been forced into it. I wondered if she'd worn it like that as a girl. Of course, not wet, but close to her head and neck. She'd probably been a sweet little girl—polite, eager to please.

"My face is old, isn't it, Al?" she said to her reflection in the mirror. Her face looked pale without make-up, but she looked like a woman in her forties, not old. "Time is passing me by. I'm going to die alone. An old spinster."

I didn't know what to say to comfort her. I couldn't tell her she reminded me of a little girl, innocent—but oh, what the world had done to her. "With your hair up you'll be back to looking like your old self again."

"Yes. My *old* self?" She turned to me. "Do you think I can ever really be like I once was?"

She was waiting for me to answer and I wanted to say yes, I really did, but it wouldn't come out. "I think you should come and stay with me for a little while," I said, guiding her down the stairs. "Rest. We'll get a, a . . . a maid? Or someone to clean . . ." My eyes roamed around the room, wondering who in the world I could ever get to take this job.

"But won't Max be there? I don't want to see him."

"I live on the top floor. *I* hardly ever see him. I have to call him on the phone to meet him in our living room."

"Al, he's going to notice I'm there. I don't want him knowing about what I've done and—"

"We won't tell him about, well, you know, everything." Was I lying? Would I tell him behind her back? I never told him what Moose did to her. How do you find words to talk about something like that? Especially to a man. But had *she*? "We'll just say we're two girlfriends who need to catch up, so we decided to have a pajama party like girls do. He won't question that. You know how men hate hearing about girl stuff. You can't stay here."

She giggled. "We'll be like girlfriends?"

"That's right. Like girlfriends."

"First, I must get my hair done. I can't go around town looking like this. What if I run into someone I know? I wonder if Mr. Pierre's Petite Salon could fit me in today. Oh. They don't take last minute appointments over there," she said, sad. "Mr. Pierre throws things when anyone wants to break one of his rules. If I call and ask him, he might get mad at me and ban me for months."

"What? No! No, no, he won't do that," I said. "*Because* he will make an exception for you." He'd better, I thought, after all the money Virginia probably spent in that guy's place. "If he doesn't give you an appointment right away, I'll go over there myself and bop 'Mr. Pierre' on his new nose."

She giggled. "You're good for me, Al."

Virginia tiptoed through the door to my apartment behind me, her fingers gripping a hunk of my coat. She was terrified she'd find Max sitting on the sofa in the living room, reading his paper. She was relieved to find he wasn't home, and so was I.

She looked good with her hair done up the way she always wore it. She looked like the Virginia I'd always known. I'd called Mr. Pierre from Virginia's house when she was upstairs packing an overnight bag. I warned him about his new nose and what would happen to it if he didn't give Virginia an appointment within the next hour. He was extremely cooperative.

We tiptoed up the kelly-green carpeted stairs to my apartment, even though tiptoeing wasn't necessary. I led the way through the locked door into my living room and then . . . I just stood there. I'd never had any guests to my apartment before. Well, Marty had come over a few times, but he wasn't a real guest. He was just my buddy. Max had come up when I first moved in to give me a few decorating tips, but after that he didn't come up much. I always met Max and Scott downstairs if we were going to get together. And besides, Virginia—she came from wealth. I remembered the first day I visited her in her mansion.

Ainsworth greeted me at the door. I mean, she actually had a real live English butler who called me madam. And inside? Oh, my! Two marble staircases swooped down into the center of the foyer. A huge chandelier hung from the high ceiling and the floor was as shiny as the one in the Metropolitan Museum of Art. When Virginia walked down the stairs from her room to get me, I remember thinking how strange it seemed that even when she was home and no one could see her, she dressed in her finest with her hair piled up on top of her head.

Virginia and I had met a lot at Schrafft's for lunch, the way ladies do, but she seemed much too elegant for me to invite to my home. Max had had her over to his part of the house a few times. I mean our place wasn't exactly a dump—living on Fourth Avenue just below Park, wasn't so bad—but I couldn't picture me having Virginia over to my upstairs apartment. *She* used to live in a mansion with servants. She was the most elegant person I knew. In a fussy sort of way. Then, a picture: I saw her standing ankle-deep in garbage, her hair a tangled mess. How do I put the two pictures together?

"Such a lovely room," Virginia said, standing near the window with the filmy yellow curtains. Nice paneling. Very colonial."

"Oh, yeah, colonial was all the rage a couple years ago. Don't know about now. Why don't you sit."

"Oh? Should I? Here? On this fluffy chair?"

"Yeah. There." I was sure the green flowers sewn on that chair were all wrong. What do I do with her? Talk furniture? I don't know anything about that. Why did Max get me into this? I looked at my watch. Much too early to go to bed.

"Oh, look," she said, "you have a nice window right next to this chair. Isn't that nice? You can see outside at the buildings."

"Yes. Nice." Now, we both sounded like two weirdos. We smiled stupidly at each other. *Talk, Al,* I told myself. *Say something fascinating, interesting. Say anything.* Those ugly pictures ran through my brain and . . . "Food!" I blurted out.

"What?" Virginia said, almost falling out of her seat.

"You must be starved."

"Oh, don't fuss."

Fuss? Fuss? I didn't have one darn thing in my Shelvadore. I never ate at home. No time. My Shelvadore was always empty. "Chinese take-out!" I shouted for no reason. "You want that?" I wished I could take it back. Virginia eating Chinese takeout really didn't seem—

"What is it?" she asked.

"Chinese takeout? You mean you've never . . . Oh, you wouldn't like it."

"How do you know? Tell me."

"Recently some Chinese restaurants in the city have been putting their food into white cardboard boxes so you can eat at home."

"How nice of them. And convenient. Such an adventure. Let's do that."

"An adventure? Really? Only . . . I'll have to go out and get it. It wouldn't take long. But would you mind being here alone?"

"Not at all. Can I watch your television set?"

"Sure. But when I first got a TV you said you'd never want one because you'd rather listen to your concert records. I don't have any concert records. Just some hot jazz and a few of the new rock and roll songs."

"Well . . ." she whispered, "I bought a TV a few years ago."

"You did?"

"Yes!" She giggled. "I keep it in my bedroom. I rather like it. Do you mind?"

"Not at all. Just let me get you the television menu. Then I'll put it on for you."

"Television menu?"

"That's what they call the menu for the takeout food." I kneeled on the rug to rummage through the end table drawer by the couch. "I guess because they expect you to watch your TV while you're eating it. Here it is." I held it out for her. "See if anything looks good to you."

―――――

When I got back with my arms filled with Chinese food, I stopped short in the doorway, frozen. Not wanting to leave Virginia alone too long, I had run all the way to the restaurant. I yelled at poor Woo Chong for going too slow, then, ran back to my apartment. It all had been totally unnecessary. I stood in the entrance of my living room, luxuriating in the sounds of Juliana singing "O Mio Babbino." Virginia had found my 78 rpm copy of the record Max and Shirl had produced before the war and she was playing it on my hi-fi. It had been such a long time since I heard Juliana sing that. I remembered how Armand at the party in Paris had said it was up to me to find a way for Juliana to sing opera to the public. Only singing opera for the public would make her complete. I walked over to the hi fi and lifted the arm off the record. Suddenly, it felt too personal to be playing it now.

"Do you mind that I listened to it?" Virginia asked.

"No. But we don't want our food getting cold." I put the record back in its

brown sleeve and laid it on top of the other records piled near the TV. "I need to change my clothes. I'll be back."

"Yes, of course, be comfortable."

I ran to my room to let the tears run while I threw on a red-and-white striped knit top and a pair of navy pedal pushers. I slid my feet into a pair of penny loafers. What a relief to be rid of the girdle and heels.

CHAPTER FIVE

"*D*id she say if she got my flowers?" Richard asked as I sipped my cold coffee at Hector's Cafeteria. I hadn't gotten much sleep. With Virginia there to remind me, the nightmares came swooping down on me. I kept being awakened by blood and flying body parts. Those dreams hadn't disturbed me in five years since the time when it all happened. I looked over at Virginia sleeping quietly on her back in the extra bed. I wondered if beyond the quiet wall of her skin and skull, there was a terror raging within that I couldn't see.

I held a pile of newspapers on my lap. A tray of silverware clanged to the floor, and I nearly jumped out of my skin as a counterman rushed to pick it up. My nerves were a frazzled mess. I hadn't heard from Max in four days. "I hate thinking of her sitting alone in that dressing room," Richard went on, "with no flowers, but who does she know in Philadelphia?"

"She got them, Richard. She said they were beautiful."

"She told you that?" Richard asked like a smitten school boy.

"Yes, she did. But I doubt she was alone in her dressing room. Juliana has a way of attracting people to herself. I'm sure if she were alone in the middle of the Sahara Desert some sheik would show up on his camel."

Richard laughed. "I suppose you're right." Then his face turned sour. "What sheik? Do you know something?"

"Relax." I was in no mood for coddling him.

He poured more syrup onto his pancakes. "I wish I'd been there with her; she told me to stay here. I had a couple of business meetings, but I could've gotten out of them. She told me not to bother myself, as if she could *ever* be a bother to me. I'm her husband for Pete's sake. I'd do anything for her."

"Including *not* going to Philly for the tryout because it would make her more nervous than she already was."

"Yes. Even that." He sighed. "She always pretends not to be nervous, but *I* know. You don't stay married to a woman for seventeen and a half years and not know all the little details she tries to hide. Did, uh, Max go to the show?"

"No. He was too busy with his clubs."

"Oh. Are you sure you won't have something to eat? Eggs? Pancakes? These pancakes are delicious."

"No, I can't eat now. I'm getting ready to read the reviews."

"I wish I were like that. Lately, every time I get anxious I *start* eating. I think it's beginning to show. This morning I had to hook my belt into the first hole. Pretty soon I'm going to need a whole new belt."

He did look a little wider, even from when I saw him in Paris. And there seemed to be more gray on the sides of his head too. He was developing into an older, doughier version of his younger self, with fat cheeks. He looked like a man who would someday make a happy grandpa, but he was married to the wrong woman for that to ever happen.

"What do they say?" he asked.

"Well, *Billboard* says *Queen for a Day* has the top Nielson ratings of any TV show on the air. And it's only been on for a month. Do you know that show?"

"Only from radio," he said. "My mother used to listen to it. I never paid much attention."

"Well, each week they have five women compete with each other by telling their sad stories into a microphone, and the one whose life is the most miserable gets a new Westinghouse washing machine or toaster or something. There's something disturbing about that, don't you think?"

"How do they decide whose life is the worst?"

"Applause meters. The audience claps for the one with the most pathetic life."

Richard shook his head. "Yes, that is disturbing. Why would anyone want to go on TV to announce to the whole world that their life is worse than anyone else's?"

"For the washing machine, I suppose."

"Small consolation. We should get back to Juliana. What do the reviews say? Have you read any of them yet?'

"No. They're here." I pulled the newspapers up from my lap and dumped them on our table. "Ready?"

"Not really." He put more pancake in his mouth.

I turned to the theater section of the *Philadelphia Inquirer*. "*Heaven is to Your Left* is One Heavenly Disaster," the headline read.

"Oh, no," Richard and I said at the same time.

I quickly skimmed the words, but I could hardly take in their meaning. "An incomprehensible book, tunes with no melody, the juvenile's legs got twisted up in each other, off-key chorus . . ." It went on and on. I literally thought I was going to be sick, until . . . "The true heavenly moments of the evening (and thank God, quite literally, they were legion) were delivered by Juliana, a relative newcomer to the stage, but a veteran singer. I looked up. "Richard, listen to this. 'She made this reviewer glad he donned his tuxedo to brave the snow and sit through that heavenly mess. For whenever Miss Juliana was on stage, be it singing, dancing, talking, or merely observing the others, the auditorium was on fire with her electricity. She made it all worthwhile. Now I know what all that Copacabana fuss has been about. May the gods above soon grant Miss Juliana a property worthy of her gifts."

"Wow." I looked up at Richard.

"Yes, wow," he agreed.

The two of us scrambled to read the other papers. Some of the actors who'd been maligned in the *Inquirer* fared better in these, but not one reviewer had anything but praise and adoration for Juliana.

I hit the metal table. "Oh, yes!"

"Our girl is on her way. Isn't she, Al?"

Our girl? This was getting weirder and weirder. I took a deep breath and said softly, "Yes, Richard, our girl is on her way."

CHAPTER SIX

"How'd she do?" Max asked, bounding into my office and onto the chair next to my desk.

"Where the hell have you been? I've been looking all over—"

"Don't curse; it's not ladylike. So, tell me how things went with Juliana."

"Do you know that Virginia is now living with me on the top floor?"

"Oh, no, that's not good. She can't stay there. Send her home."

"I can't. I found her living in the most appalling squalor." I was doing it. Telling Max what Virginia didn't want me to tell him. But what else could I do?

"Squalor? Virginia? Impossible. Why?"

"She needs someone to look after her. She's never lived completely alone before. She's always at least had servants. You know, people. Virginia has money. Hire someone. Only . . ."

"What?"

"That may not be enough. She may need some kind of doctor—a doctor for her head."

"What on earth for? Virginia has always been a levelheaded girl."

"Everyone is going to psychoanalysts these days. She might like it.

Having someone to listen to her. She feels lonely. And well, even you said she was acting crazy."

"I didn't mean that literally. She just kept calling me and—"

"Interrupting you? And how *is* Scott?"

"Fine."

"You're sure?"

"Very. I have warm feelings for Virginia."

"Well, you're going to have to take those *warm* feelings and get her out of my rooms and into her *own* home. I'm not used to roommates. And maybe a doctor."

"Well, I know some gentlemen who might know some doctors like that."

"Gentlemen, huh? What kind?"

"Gentlemen. What's the matter with you?"

"Just be sure you appreciate Scott. You won't get better than him."

"Tell me about Juliana and Philly."

"Get a load of these." I jumped up and lifted the papers from the top of my file cabinet and flung them down onto my desk.

"Good?" he asked, picking up the *Inquirer*.

"No. Great."

He quickly thumbed to the theater section and read the review; his face glowed with pride. He picked up the *Philadelphia Daily News* and read. "This is wonderful. I hope by the time they bring the show to New York they've got a cast that can properly support her."

"Harry Fielding will take care of that, but Max, you need to keep an eye on Schuyler. Make sure he doesn't try any funny business."

"Oh, he won't do anything now that he's got these reviews. That's all he ever wanted. To reclaim his reputation. As long as he produces the show in New York better than he did in Philly, it won't be to his advantage to mess with Juliana."

"You're sure?"

"Have a little faith." He moved on to read another review.

"It's hard working with Lucille."

"Why?" He put the paper back in the pile. "Do you think she's the one who's working with Schuyler?"

"She might be. I'm suspicious of everything she does. If she brings me a newspaper article, which is her job, I wonder why she chose that *particular* time to bring it to me. If she calls me on my dictograph, which is the only way she has of contacting me from her office, I get afraid she's taping the call."

"Oh, come on, how could she do that?"

"There are those special dictograph telephones that the police use to spy on criminals. Maybe—"

"Do you really think Lucille could install that type of equipment on her own, in your office, with no one noticing? Come on. You're getting carried away."

"She could've done it while I was in Paris. You weren't here every day."

"I was here a lot. Training her."

"See!"

"What?"

"She has all the inside information to—"

"What inside information? Nothing's been taken from the safe."

"You didn't give her the combination?"

"Of course not. She doesn't know anything about that part of the business. I would never share that with her. Lucille is a sweet, harmless girl who is a little bit goofy, and you're letting Schuyler unbalance you. You need to be calm under these circumstances."

"You're right. Of course, you're right."

"I always am."

"But—don't you think Lucille is a little *too* sweet?"

"That's ridiculous."

"You see, you see, sometimes I think I'm going nuts with all this. Every strange sound I hear through the phone wires, especially when I'm talking to Juliana, makes me jump. Juliana and I never talk, uh . . . well, you know, intimately on the phone, but I still imagine someone might . . . Through the whole call I worry I might have left the privacy button off, even though I'm staring at it and can see that I didn't. Then, there's Bertha. She's always wanting to do things for me."

"And that's not a good thing?" Max asked.

"No. She's not to supposed to be here in the afternoon, but there she is. The first person I see whenever I arrive. I can hardly bear saying hello to her, but I force myself so she doesn't catch on that I suspect her. Recently, I suggested she not arrive at the club until evening, but she said she enjoyed being near me. Don't you think *that's* suspicious?"

"No. I think it sounds like she's hot for you."

"Nonsense. She's straight. She keeps telling me she 'understands me,' a woman in my position. I want her to *stop* understanding me. Immediately."

Max burst into unrestrained laughter.

"Oh, you're no help at all."

Chapter Seven

MARCH 1956

*A*fter I got off the subway at Forty-Second, I sloshed through the piles of snow toward the Henry Miller Theater on Forty-Third, where Juliana was rehearsing. For two days, we'd had a steady blanketing of snow so that now the streets and the rooftops were covered with lumpy white mountains. The snow on the sidewalks was beginning to turn gray and brown from dog walkers and their dogs. A few cars were still buried under a heavy weight of ice that their owners hadn't managed to dig out yet. I pulled my serviceable wool coat tighter around me to block out the cold.

Back from Philly, Juliana was rehearsing for the show's opening that was only a week away. They now had a whole new script *and* a new musical director and choreographer. Plus, Marvin Van Ville had been hired to replace the male lead. This was quite a coup for Juliana, because Van Ville was a popular Broadway matinee idol, adored by the press as well as his fans.

I'd heard it said that it took Marvin hours to leave the theater after a show because on the other side of the stage door were hordes of women screaming his name and shaking autograph books at him. Unlike some Broadway stars, Marvin didn't try to escape. He genuinely enjoyed their attention and generously gave to these women. *Variety* quoted him as saying, "It's part of the job, a duty."

Tommie also was called in at the last moment, to replace the second lead. Special, special Tommie flying through the Stage Door Canteen with me during the war. I hadn't seen him since the month before I left for Paris, and I hadn't seen Juliana since mid-February, so I was excited to get to this rehearsal.

I stomped my way into the lobby, slipping on the slick black-and-white marble floor and waving my arms around to keep me from falling over. Apple, the assistant stage manager, ran over and grabbed me. "Hey!" He set me upright. "You okay?"

"Fine. Boots wet. Imagine. Snow like this now. It's almost April!" I grumbled as I walked through the bright blue inner foyer that led to the orchestra seating area. I pulled off my boots, threw my overcoat over one of the back-row seats, and headed down the center aisle toward Bobby McClaren, Tommie's wife. He'd told us he was going to marry her that weekend of Marty's and my graduation, and he did. His hit opening night at Café Society, Uptown, came back to me.

I looked up, taking in the beauty of the architecture that surrounded me. The walls were covered with amber brocade and the seats were similarly tapestried. Above me was an impossibly high ceiling with an ornate chandelier hanging from it. The two balconies lifted up behind me and seemed to melt into the ceiling. On two sides, I was surrounded by box seats.

I hurried down to Bobby sitting in the center aisle, knitting. She was round and short with stubby little legs that poked out of her flared shirtwaist dress. She was a pretty girl, not yet thirty, with a soft feminine face framed by bangs and short bouncy hair. In between stitches, she looked up at Tommie, who was running lines with Abby Warner, the ingenue. I didn't see Juliana.

"Hey, Bobby," I whispered as I slid into the seat next to her. "How's it been going?"

"Tommie's terrified," she whispered back. "How can they expect him to prepare in only a week?"

"Don't worry. Tommie's a trooper," I said.

"I'm not worried about him. I'm worried about *me*. I was up all night running lines with him. When I *finally* got to sleep, he began singing scales."

No matter how much Bobby complained about Tommie, she was the totally devoted wife. Right after Tommie and she got married, she gave up her own film ambitions to devote herself completely to Tommie's career.

When Tommie and Bobby stood next to each other, they looked like those comic strip characters, Mutt and Jeff. Tommie was tall and slender, his gestures delicate, while Bobby was short and stocky. It was kind of funny seeing them next to each other.

I met Bobby at their wedding in LA. Max, Marty, Scott, and I went. Bobby and I hit it off right away, and I had gone out a few more times to visit them. Tommie and Bobby were a pretty typical lavender couple.

"Take ten," the stage manager, Ron, called, and Tommie floated off the stage, his arms flapping like a bird as he tiptoed gracefully toward the two of us sitting in the center aisle. "Al! Al," he cried. I stood, and we embraced.

"Oh, honey, I *have* missed you," he said. "Kissy, kissy." He took me into his arms and we kissed each other's cheeks.

"Enough of that," Bobby said, putting down her knitting to stand with us. "He's *my* honey bunch."

Tommie released me and brought Bobby close to him. "Hey, sweet pea." He kissed her on the end of her nose.

"You were damn good, buddy," Bobby said and punched him in the arm.

"Ow!" Tommy grabbed his arm.

"Oh, stop. It was just a love pat, petunia. To keep you in shape. You've got to watch those high notes. Your voice isn't built to go that high. They should rewrite that first act song for your voice."

"I can handle it, Mommy."

"We'll go over it tonight."

They gave each other quick kisses on the lips. "I simply must have a smoke"—he skipped back toward the stage and dramatically held a hand to his forehead—"or I shall perish."

"They're not good for your voice!" Bobby yelled after him with the tone of an umpire calling, "Strike three. You're out."

Tommie and Bobby had bought a split-level on the outskirts of LA before coming to New York so they'd have a real home to go back to after all the New York hotel living was done.

Ron, the stage manager, called everyone back to work. That's when I finally saw Juliana. She stepped onto the stage from the wings, and my breath got stuck somewhere between my lungs and my throat. She moved toward the center of the stage, and my heart fluttered to the sound of her heels lightly clicking against the wood. She had her hair done up in a bouffant. And, oh, how lovely she looked in her Evan Piccone pencil skirt and double-breasted blouse, the pointy collar sitting up against her neck, highlighting the short hair in back and the small silver earrings sitting delicately on her earlobes. I wanted to run up on stage and pull her into my arms and . . . She wasn't even looking at me. I wondered if she knew I was there, but . . . No, we couldn't risk even a careless glance among our own. The whole world had suddenly become more dangerous.

She stood speaking to Tommie. He was playing the next-door neighbor. The rehearsal pianist ran her fingers over the keys as Stan Devenbach entered from the side door. So, *he* was to be the musical director. This was not going to go over well with Juliana. It wasn't going over well with *me*, either. He must have been a last-minute hire, like this morning, because I'd heard nothing about it. Stan was the musical director who had walked out on us on Juliana's first opening night at the Copa. Johnny, her pianist, got blind drunk an hour before she was to go on. We were counting on Stan to find a replacement, but instead he walked out, took advantage of the escape clause he made us put in his contract, and left us with nothing. We fixed it, of course, or I did, but he was not someone either of us were too happy to see.

Juliana stiffened as Stan approached the stage in his usual three-piece suit, checking his pocket watch as he went.

"No, Harry," Juliana said firmly to the director. "No! Get this man away from me. I cannot work with him."

"Look, Julie," Harry said, rising from his front row aisle seat. He rolled up the sleeves on his striped shirt and poked his thumbs through his suspenders. "All we have is a week. Stan's a veteran. He's the only one I know who can pull this together that fast."

"I cannot—will not work with that man." She threw her script on the floor and walked off.

Harry turned toward the back of the room. "Dan?"

Dan Schuyler had just come in. He hadn't even finished unbuttoning his coat. "I'll take care of it, Harry." He pulled off his overcoat and scarf and threw them across a couple of theater seats in the back. Hurrying down the center aisle, he adjusted his tie and went out through a side door. Why didn't *Harry* go to Juliana? Harry was one of us. Was it because Dan was the producer, or did he know Schuyler had the power to control her? Could the others know? The radiator crackled, pouring in too much heat; still, I shivered, thinking of Juliana facing Dan alone.

Through the silence of waiting, the radiator banged and Bobby's knitting needles clicked; no one even tried to make conversation. We just sat there with our own thoughts, waiting.

Juliana returned to the stage. She bent over and picked up her script. "Shall we begin?"

"Yes. Yes, of course," Harry said, hurrying to stand near the apron of the stage, obviously wanting to get beyond this horribly awkward moment. "Stan?" he said, turning to Devenbach, who sat in a front row center seat.

Stan stood, pulled on the edge of his suit jacket, and said, "Let's begin with, 'Anytime You Want.'"

The rehearsal pianist played the introduction and Juliana began to sing. The sounds she made were like liquid magic. Despite all the strain, her voice kept growing stronger and purer.

Dan, leaning against the side doorsill, straightened, clapping. "Delightful, dear." He approached the stage. "I wish I could stay for the whole rehearsal, but alas, I have several meetings to attend. Hopefully they will do the show good." He hurried down the center aisle, scooped up his coat and scarf, and went out the back.

As soon as he was gone, the tension sizzling in the room lifted like a collective sigh of relief. I hadn't noticed it filling up the place till it was gone. It was the unconscious tension we often felt when a "normal" we weren't sure of walked among us. Unconscious until said normal was gone.

Stan called for a rehearsal of the duet with Marvin. Marvin Van Ville was an attractive man in his late forties with a sweep of black hair and a touch of gray at the temples to make him look distinguished. I think he planned it that way. Marvelous magic came in bottles.

Marvin and Juliana sang together, their voices melding and harmonizing. The chorus boys and girls stood behind them, singing different lyrics. Then Juliana and Marvin's voices were no longer harmonizing. They were having an argument in song. The chorus boys sang with Marvin, while the girls sang with Juliana. Stan stopped them a few times, gave some direction that I couldn't hear, and then they began again.

Bobby elbowed me. "She's good, hey?"

Ron, the stage manager, called the break for lunch, which was my cue to get back to the office and get something done. I was working on getting a hot singer or a hot group to commit to doing a few weeks at the club. We needed somebody big to get through our slump but negotiating a fee that didn't sink us was becoming a problem. I'd been thinking of the Four Aces. I just loved their "Love is a Many Splendored Thing." I wished Jule and I could dance together to that. The Four Aces would be expensive for the Haven right now. I wondered about the Four Lads. Their songs were climbing the charts or . . . maybe the Four Preps. What was this thing with four? But yes! The Preps might work. They were new, practically unknown. Practically unknown won't do anything for our audience problem. No good. I had to get back to the office and figure something out. As I got up from my seat, a newsboy whizzed in, stomping melting snow all over the rug. "*Tip Off!*" he called out, waving a thin magazine. "Brand new! Different! Not a gossip rag! Only the facts. Researched facts. Get 'em here while they're hot. Filled with shocking behind the scenes stories of Katharine Hepburn, Winston Churchill, Gloria Vanderbilt, Margaret O'Brien."

A few of us lined up to give the kid our quarter and get a copy of this new entertainment magazine that was supposed to deliver only the "facts." Most of the actors and crew were more practical and had run off to get food. The fearless director, Harry, was one of the first out the door. I was eager to read "Why Katharine Hepburn Gave the Roman Wolves the Razz." Now that sounded like a piece of solid investigative journalism. I slid my copy into my briefcase to be read over lunch in my office. I was pulling on my boots when Ron called out to the few of us that were left. "Hey, kids! Did you see what's in here?" He signaled us to meet him around the piano and he hurried down the proscenium steps. Juliana was already reading the magazine in her chair on stage and didn't get up to join the rest.

I hopped a few steps in one boot to get to my briefcase. I slipped the newsprint magazine out and skimmed the titles of the articles until I came to "Why They Call Broadway the 'Gay' White Way.'" My heart fell into my stomach. I spun around just in time to see Juliana giving me a glance before quickly looking down at her paper again. The group by the piano were giggling. I thumbed my way through the article, breathless, terrified I'd find Juliana and my name in there.

"They don't mention names in there, do they?" I heard Marvin whisper.

I hurried to join Ron, Tommie, Bobby, Marvin, and Apple.

"Ron said, "I wonder which show the guy means in this paragraph? 'Three shows which were on Broadway within the past year were completely dominated by deviates.'"

"Only three?" Apple, the assistant stage manager, a safe straight, laughed. "So, tell me which one *wasn't* dominated by you guys?"

"No!" Tommie squawked, jumping up and down. "Deviates in the theater? I'm shocked."

Subdued laughter.

I kept looking toward the back to be sure Dan Schuyler hadn't shown up while skimming ahead through the article, looking for Juliana's and my name.

"This guy claims," Ron whispered, "there's a producer's wife who goes around asking pretty chorus girls to her house for lunch. If the girl doesn't accept, the next time her producer-husband is casting a show, that little beauty is plain out of dumb luck. Who do you think that is?" Hey, Juliana! You know this woman?" Ron asked.

"How would I know people like that? You know perfectly well I live the dull life of an ordinary housewife."

"Sure, Julie honey, sure," Ron said, and the others giggled into their hands.

"Oh, no!" Tommie said, jumping up and down and flapping his hands. "They're calling us the 'lace pantie set.' Isn't that adorable?"

"Stop!" Marvin said, stomping his foot against the floor. "I don't want to listen to any more of this childish nonsense. I'll come back when you're ready to behave as professionals." He charged off the set fists swinging as if he were trying to look like Mr. Universe heading for a Muscle magazine photo shoot.

Everyone broke into raucous laughter, but as the laughter slowly subsided, a sadness snuck into the room. We weren't expecting it. Well, at least we had each other, I thought, because we knew most "normals," "straights," "jams"—whatever we called them—would never knowingly invite any of us into their homes.

"It's beginning to feel like a funeral in here," Ron said. "Everybody. Out. Have lunch and don't come back late or sad. Remember we're sposed to be gay. Act like it."

———

I picked up a brisket on rye at the Carnegie Deli on my way back to the office. When I entered the Haven, I found Bertha there as always, but she wasn't alone. She stood near my office door, giggling with one of her girlfriends. "Do you believe this book?" she said to her.

"What are you doing in front of my door?" I asked so firmly I scared myself.

The book flew out of Bertha's chubby hands. The other girl stood frozen. "We, we were just, just . . ." Bertha stammered.

I bent over to retrieve the book. In large yellow letters across the front ran the title, *Queer Affair*. Two women with low-cut blouses, one running her hand through the other's hair, were pictured under the title. Above the title, it read, *"Theirs was a passion no man could share. The novel that dares to tell the truth about perverse love."*

I swallowed down my terror and looked Bertha straight in the eyes. "I believe you dropped your book, Bertha." I held it out to her.

"It's not mine," she squealed, pushing it back at me. "It's disgusting."

"Is it? I thought you were reading it because you're queer." I could hardly get the word passed my lips.

"No!" Bertha backed away from me, horrified.

I pushed the book at the other girl. "Yours?"

"No." The girl shook her head, on the verge of tears.

I turned back to Bertha. "Should I report the kind of filth you bring into the club to Max?"

"Please, no," Bertha pleaded. "I need this job."

"It's illegal, you know, for homosexuals to work in establishments that sell liquor. Maybe you *should* be fired."

"No. Please. I'm not one of those. I'm not. I'm not. I can't lose this job. My mother would kill me. We need the money."

"Then take this garbage out into the street and never let me see you bring something like it back into the Haven ever again." I pushed the book at Bertha's hands.

"Don't make me take it," she whimpered. "What if someone sees me?"

"You brought it in. You'll take out. With your own two hands. You walk out that door"—I pointed—"past Giorgio and throw it into the trash receptacle in the street. Now!"

"Here's the bag you brought it in," the other girl offered.

I grabbed the bag from her hand. "No! Take it like that."

Bertha took the book from me and held it in front of her as if it were a bomb about to explode. "Be sure no one catches you with it," I said. "They're liable to think you're a dyke."

I'd never seen Bertha run so fast. The other girl stood there frozen. "Go!" I shouted at her "Before I call your mother and tell her"—I whispered—"you're queer." I didn't know if she was young enough to have a mother who'd care, but she ran out the door anyway.

Shaking, I opened my office door, locked it, and pulled down the shade. I pushed my nails into my wood desk. I remembered that time before Paris. I was auditioning a girl for the new show. Ethel, yes, Ethel was her name. I was surprised I remembered it. She sang and danced for me. And just as I was about to end the audition, she took off all her clothes and tried to seduce me. I managed to get her back into her clothes and out of the club, but as I watched her go, I turned to see Bertha standing there. Had she watched the whole thing? I didn't do anything about it. But how might Bertha have interpreted that? That night she gave me a strange smile and said, "I know you're not one of *those* types of women." And the way she said those words made my skin itch. Now, I knew. Bertha must be the one. My betrayer. She must be in cahoots with Schuyler.

Tears slid down my face and a panic gripped me. I felt completely vulnerable, naked, and about to collapse. I wanted to crawl under my desk. Disappear. And more tears came, and it took every bit of strength to not cry out to some God I used to believe in as a child. A God of love who cared about me. Where was that God now? The one who gave a damn about deviates? Was there such a God?

———

I sat frozen at my desk for what may have been hours. I do remember watching the cold sun gradually disappear from the window as everything turned to black. My only thought—it was Bertha. Bertha was the one. Our betrayer. Bertha. All that fawning over me and snooping around. *She* must've left that book on my desk before I left for Paris. From what she said, it sounded like she was providing financial support for her mother. Schuyler probably paid her to spy on me. I shivered at the thought. Trust no one. That must be my slogan from now on.

There was a desperate knocking on the door, jarring me from my numbness. Someone was on the other side of that shade. I waited, holding my breath, hoping they'd go away. The knocking persisted. I quickly wiped my eyes with my soggy handkerchief and threw it in my purse. A strange fear grabbed me, like there was some dark specter on the other side of that door, something that wanted to hurt me . . . or worse. My heart thumping, I slowly raised the brown shade and on the other side of the window—Virginia and Mercy, giggling and still knocking.

"Let us in," Mercy's voice came muffled through my door.

I unlocked the door and pulled it open, plastering a smile on my face. "Hi."

"Come on, let's go," Mercy said. "We're taking you out."

They both wore long winter coats buttoned to the neck. Mercy's hat was a small platter type while Virginia's was more elaborate, with a peak pointing upward. The two of them showing up at my door seemed very odd. I hadn't spoken to Mercy much since I got back from Paris. All my energy had been focused on the "Schuyler" problem. All else had faded from existence. Oh and, of course, there was the Virginia problem too. But I didn't see her all that much, even though she was still living with me. Only enough for her to greet me when I got home at four in the morning and to complain that I was never home, and my long hours weren't good for me, and she was lonely, and on and on until I finally collapsed into my bed. It was probably like having an annoying wife.

"I'm really not up to going out tonight," I sighed, my heart feeling like it weighed two tons. "It's thoughtful of you both to come get me, but . . . Please don't think I don't appreciate it, but I have so much paperwork."

"Enough work," Virginia said. "You work too much. Put on your coat."

She grabbed my coat from the rack and started aggressively stuffing my arms into the armholes, almost hurting me. "No, look," I objected, "please, this is kind, but—"

"Your hat," Mercy said, plopping the round navy blue hat on the crown of my head.

"First," Virginia said, grabbing my hand and pulling my listless self out of the office, "we have special tickets."

"To what?"

"You'll see," Mercy said.

"And afterwards," Virginia continued, "we're taking you out for a nice dinner, so we can talk about it. We have reservations at Longchamp's. It's simply scandalous to eat at a restaurant that elegant and at night without men, but who cares?" She threw her hands into the air. "Throw caution to the winds. We're going to be daring tonight. It'll be a delicious girls' night out. That's right isn't it, Mercy?"

"You betcha', as Shirl would say."

"We're going to talk about what?" I asked.

"The thing we have the special tickets for."

"But I can't stay out that late. I have two shows to get through later tonight."

"Lucille said she would cover for you. She's just as worried about you as we are."

"Is she?" I said, doubtfully. Then I remembered it was *Bertha*, not Lucille who betrayed me. I'd exonerated Lucille. Distrusting Lucille had become a habit.

Mercy and Virginia walked me out past the Haven's doors. We stood under the awning. "You haven't been up to anything since you got back from Paris," Virginia said. "I don't know what that Juliana did to you, but—"

"Nothing! She didn't do anything to me," I said, angrier than I expected to be. "She was wonderful. More wonderful than, than . . ." I had to stop, or I would start crying again.

"I'm sorry," Virginia said, sincerely. "Sometimes I say things I don't mean." She touched my hand.

Mercy left us and marched past Giorgio to the curb, whistled through her fingers, and yelled, "Taxi!"

"Mercy!" Virginia and I both exclaimed, shocked. Giorgio, whose job she'd just usurped, looked pretty shocked too.

"I've never heard you make so much noise before," I said.

"And on the street," Virginia said. "What has happened to our demure, little Mercy?"

"Shirl taught me that." Mercy beamed with pride. The cab slid into the curb. "So I'd never get stranded when she wasn't with me." She threw open the door with the force of a truck driver and ordered, "Get in."

"Where are we going?" I asked.

"Get in," Virginia said, giving me a push.

We all slid in with me in the center. "Should we tell her?" Virginia asked, leaning over me toward Mercy.

"Yes!" I said.

"Oh, not that," Mercy said. "We're not telling you where we're going until we get there. You mean the other. Don't you, Virginia?"

"Yes. Should we?"

"Go ahead. Why don't you do it."

"Tell me what?"

"I'm going to live with Mercy and Shirl!" Virginia declared.

"You are?"

"Yes, she is," Mercy said. "We've got that extra room no one's using. I'm going to clean it out and she can have it. And since Shirl and I aren't out as much as you, Virginia won't get so lonely."

"I'm sorry I made you feel alone."

"No," Virginia said, tapping my knee. "You have your career. Mercy and I live more quietly so it'll be a better fit. And their TV has a remote control!"

The cab took us into the campus of Brooklyn College. Walking past the bold buildings and the sculpted lawns reminded me of the simplicity of my life at City College. I recalled my first meeting with Marty when he saved me from being trampled by the cops. The things we'd done together, and the talks we'd had, came tumbling back. To cover my sadness, I laughed extra loud with Virginia and Mercy.

As we were about to enter the college auditorium, I noted a large poster propped up on an easel. It said, "TONIGHT Dr. Murray Banks Speaks On, 'Our Sex Life: Integrating the Kinsey Report—Male and Female.'"

"What are we doing here?" I asked.

"It's supposed to be very enlightening, and funny too," Virginia said.

We situated ourselves in the center on the hard wood seats that school auditoriums always seemed to have. Warmed by the heat, we squiggled out of our winter coats. The auditorium was filling up fast. Male and female couples came in, and so did quite a few small groups of women like us who chattered and giggled. This was something of a daring adventure. To come out on a weekday evening to a school auditorium and listen to a man, a psychologist, talk about sex. I'd never heard of such a thing. If only I'd been in a more festive mood.

We didn't have to wait long before Dr. Murray Banks, a pleasant-looking young man in a gray suit and tie, walked onto the stage. There was polite applause as he sat casually on a high stool to address us.

"When the Kinsey Report for Males first came out," he began, "I saw a woman on the subway reading it. I asked her how it was, and she said, 'There's no plot, but lots of action.'"

The audience laughed.

"Most people are sexual cripples," Dr. Murray continued. "Commentators are often criticizing Dr. Alfred Kinsey's work because they think this statistic or that statistic isn't correct, but Dr. Kinsey's great contribution has nothing to do with statistics. It makes no difference if the percentage of women having premarital sex is 20 percent or 80 percent or any other such statistic. Kinsey's great contribution was bringing sex out of the basement and letting us talk about it in the light of day."[1]

I looked around the auditorium. People were leaning forward, hanging onto every syllable. He went on to define terms like orgasm and coitus without hesitation or a blush. People giggled, but they didn't walk out. Dr. Murray said he *approved* of masturbation. "There is no evidence to indicate that masturbation causes blindness. Most boys, 98 percent, and a majority of girls, 64 percent, do it, and it is healthy. A preparation for marriage."

Virginia hid her eyes behind her gloves, and I wondered if that gesture revealed a guilty conscience. But I couldn't picture her doing it. She was too proper. There was quite a lot of tittering and naysaying coming from the seats around us, but this guy just went on.

He explained that men have more extramarital sex than women because women have a natural instinct to take care of children and build a home. They can't be running around with all the bucks in town and do that. Since I never felt any kind of "instinct" to have children and make a home, I wondered where I fit. Just a "deviate" I guessed.

Then he used the word "homosexuality" right out loud from the stage of a college auditorium, and I gripped the arms of my chair. "Sigmund Freud, the great psychoanalyst," he said, "has told us that we all have some amount of homosexuality in us" —*Really?* — "only some people have more than others."[1] My heart thumped in terror, and I looked around to be sure we weren't about to be raided. "Some people have quite a lot of homosexuality in them, and that makes them exclusively attracted to people of their own sex. There is nothing wrong with that. They do not deserve society's condemnation, or pity." He never once used words like pervert, deviate, or queer, or even medical terms like invert, third sex, or lesbian. He accepted us as equals. I couldn't stop staring at him. Mercy leaned over and whispered, "This is our surprise. I heard about him on the radio. Of course, the religious folks and even other psychologists claim his books and talks are evil plots to destroy society, but—"

"We can't talk about this at Longchamp's," I whispered back, still staring at this man who must've been an alien from outer space. "If someone heard us, we'd be arrested." Mercy and Virginia giggled. I couldn't join them; I was filling up with too much gratitude. For those few moments in that college auditorium, listening to that doctor's words, I almost felt safe. Like I was a part of the human race.

"Who we got lined up for tonight?" Max asked, bursting into my office. Lately, he'd been hanging around the Haven more than usual.

"I gave you the schedule last week," I told him. "I booked Johnnie Ray for the early show all month to bring in the teen crowd and then—"

Max threw himself into the chair next to my desk. "Johnnie Ray? He hasn't had a hit since '51, and he drinks. Are you sure?"

"Yeah, I am, Max," I said, with anger seeping into my voice. "He's not coming cheap. 'Just Walkin' in the Rain' is at number two, headed for number one, probably by the end of the week. "And when Johnnie sings 'Cry,' we're going have to peel the teenaged girls off the floor. Teenaged girls come with teenaged boys with money to impress them. Our reservations list is filled to capacity, which hasn't happened in a long time, and since when did you stop trusting me?"

"I haven't. I haven't." He leaned forward in his chair and laid his forehead in the palm of his hand. "It's just . . . business has been . . . well, you know and . . . I've had thoughts that maybe we should close the Haven and concentrate on the Mt. Olympus."

"No! You can't. The Haven's your dream. You made it my dream.

We're on Swing Street. The Haven's our baby. What would I do without her?"

"You'd work at the Olympus with me."

"No. That's no good. I built the Haven up from the bottom. *You* gave her to me. You think it's my fault she's in trouble, don't you?"

"No. We're struggling at the Olympus too, but maybe if we concentrate on one place—"

"No. I can pull her out of this slump. I know I can. Give me more time. I can do it. We're on Swing Street."

"Swing Street," he sighed. He put his hand on top of mine like we were talking about our teenaged kid who was going astray. "It's killing me, Al, but things are not the same. Not like the old days. There are more parking lots in this area now than night clubs. And all those shuttered clubs: Three Deuces. Famous Door. Sometimes I wonder if we'll be next."

"You can't think like that. I can pull us out of this. I know we're losing money, but . . ." It was the first time I had said it out loud, and a chill ran across my back. "Johnnie'll be good tonight. *I'm* going to make everything turn out all right again. You'll see. We can't lose the Haven."

"Who've you got for the late show?"

"The Bonnie Sisters."

"The Bonnie Sisters? Who the hell are they?"

"They had that hit last year, 'Cry Baby.' Well, it wasn't a top hit, but it got to number eighteen. And they *are* local girls. Our audience likes that."

"How come I've never heard of them?"

"Sister groups are hot right now, only . . ."

"Only?"

"Only—they're not really sisters. They're nurses who work at Bellevue."

"Oh, Al, they're nobody."

"No, they're not. You shouldn't say a terrible thing like that about anybody, but . . . these were discovered by Arthur Godfrey's Talent Show! TV, Max!"

"Okay. Maybe they'll work out."

I couldn't tell him yet that after hiring Johnnie, I was running low on money for this month's show. He'd find out soon enough.

"Okay," he said. "I'll leave it to you. You're the one with the college education."

"And don't forget Johnnie Ray comes with Dorothy Kilgallen. Whatever strange relationship those two may be having, she'll give him a good review. We're going to pull out of this slump and be on top again. You'll see." I crossed my fingers behind my back.

"I know," he said. His voice sounded tired. He pulled himself up straight in his chair. "Johnnie Ray being with Dorothy sure *is* a strange combo. First, the kid's only twenty-five and she's got to be what? Fifty?"

"I don't think she's *that* old."

"Well, what about her husband? Doesn't *he* mind?"

"She never seemed to mind his extracurricular activities or all the girls he got in trouble. Jiminy, he could've at least used protection."

"No, couldn't. He's a Catholic. Go forth and multiply. The part I don't get is Johnnie is such an obvious queen."

"Obvious to us. Not so obvious to straights. Remember those teenaged girls who'll be fainting for him tonight? The straights may hate us, but they can't recognize us even when we're sitting in their laps."

"I know, but Dorothy's no fool. She's in the business. She must know. So, what's she doing with him?"

"Providing cover? Hoping to change him? Who knows? Any way you look at it, it'll be great for us. Be happy, Max. Be happy the Haven isn't going to close its doors."

"At least not tonight." He sighed.

"Never."

"My little optimist." He headed for the door.

"Max."

He stopped but didn't turn back to face me. "Yeah?"

"I'm going to fire Bertha. I think—no, I know she's the one who's working with Schuyler against us."

"Then, you *can't* fire her." He shut my door and rushed back to the chair next to my desk. "If you're right, if Bertha really is working with him, then you must *never* fire her."

"Why?"

"Remember when Tallulah Bankhead's maid stole thousands of dollars of her jewels?"

"No."

"You really must pay more attention to gossip. Tallulah was about to have the maid arrested when the woman threatened to give the vivid details of Talu's, shall we say, rather creative sex life to the press. Things our people know about her, but the public doesn't; things like her now a man, now a woman sexuality and other sordid activities, such as not always wearing clothes when she gives a dinner party and the cocaine. It would've ruined her career, so she kept the maid in her employ and never told the authorities. If you think Bertha's the one, then you can never let her know you suspect her, and you certainly cannot fire her. Our business is shaky enough."

"Well, what the heck *am* I supposed to do with her?"

"Relax for one. Then contain the situation. Be extremely careful about what she sees and what you say around her."

"That's like trying to run this place with a gun at my head."

"Exactly. Don't forget that image."

As I predicted, our room was packed. We'd sold standing room too, so I had to push my way through the mob gathered at the back and around the tables. I wore a blue short-sleeved dress with a slight flair and white polka dots. I stood in the middle of a cluster of weeping teenagers. Johnnie Ray was singing his top hit, "Cry," which meant he was crawling on the stage floor, pulling at his hair and crying real tears as he sang about the girl who left him. Teenaged girls screamed, the boys smoked and tried to look cool; a few combed back their pompadours in memory of James Dean, but most sported crewcuts, or the side parted combed-back style that Max and Scott wore. Max had a big grin on his face as he gave me a thumbs up.

Giorgio, our doorman, tapped my arm. "Yes," I said, getting his drift right away. I *should* know what he meant. We'd been doing our duo routine for six years. Giorgio went back out to manage the door while I hurried to the office. I'd already prepared the envelopes, so all I needed to do was get them out of the safe. I walked back through the main room, pushing past the dense crowd, occasionally getting elbowed in the ribs. Dorothy Kilgallen sat up front. She looked as hormonally excited as the teenaged girls. I gave her a quick smile as I passed her. I must've been in the back when she first came in. She was sensitive about not being acknowledged, so I knew I'd have to make it up to her later.

I pushed past the front door and stood under the awning with Giorgio. "Where'd they go? They're usually right out front."

"There." He pointed.

I ran down the three shallow steps to the sidewalk where the cop car was parked in front of the truck. That truck'd be getting a ticket tonight for parking in my guys' favorite spot. Chunk, sitting in the passenger seat, rolled down his window. I bent toward him and held out the two envelopes. He took both and gave one to Murray sitting behind the wheel. I was about to run back inside—it was freezing out —when Murray said, "Wait! Dis ain't enough."

"It's the same as always."

"I know," Murray said, leaning his elbow on the steering wheel as the motor hummed. "Dat's da problem."

"Startin' today, we gotta have double," Chunk said. 'Less'n you don't give no damn 'bout what happens to yer place."

"Of course, I care what happens to this place. You know that. What are you talking about? We've been doing business for six years."

"Some unsav'ry el'ments could start frequentin' yer club," Murray said. "Ya know, immoral types, sissy homos and lessies. Ya don't want da likes a *dem* invadin' your club. It's against de law to serve 'em, ya know."

"I'm not new at this." I was growing impatient with this game they were playing. "What are you getting at?"

"If we found dem types comin' in here, we'd have no cherse but to close ya down. And we'd hate doin' dat to *you*, Al." He put his hand over his heart on his badge. "We got lots of affection fer ya, don't we, Chunk?"

"Sure do," Chunk said, his hand over his heart. "Lotsa affection, but business is business. Ya know how dat goes, Al?"

"What's this about? What's changed?"

"We heard yer business ain't so sound," Murray said.

"We're not going out of business. If that's what you mean. Did you see the crowd we have in there tonight?"

"Yeah. But what about next mont' or de mont' after dat? Here. Read. Tomorrow's *Journal-American*." He thrust a newspaper at me. "We'll be back tomorrow for the second half."

"Two in one week? You've never . . ."

Murray turned the key in the ignition and the car bucked. I moved back from the window as he pointed the wheel away from the curb. They forgot to give that truck a ticket.

I shivered—I guess with cold—and ran back into the club. I stood in the foyer and held up the *Journal*. It was folded open to Kilgallen's column, "The Voice of Broadway." I read:

"What popular swinging night club may not be
swinging much longer if the crowds stay away?"

How could she know about our financial problems? Only Max, Shirl, and I knew. It was top secret among only us. I didn't even tell Juliana. An article like this could create just what we were trying to avoid. Other papers could start nosing around and . . . Max was inside being happy, and I wanted him to stay that way for as long as possible. I snaked my way around and through the tables and teenagers that choked the aisles. I pushed my way toward Dorothy Kilgallen. Johnnie hung onto the microphone, almost swallowing it, as he sang "Don't Blame Me." Boys escorted their girls to the dance floor for this slow dance. I had to make it up to her for not welcoming her when she first came in, get back into her good graces, ask her to lunch, and convince her to print a retraction. As I drew close to Dorothy's table, I stopped short. Bertha was standing at her side. Dorothy was nodding at Bertha while trying to watch Johnnie on stage at the same time. Bertha handed Dorothy an envelope. Dorothy unsnapped her handbag and placed the envelope inside. She drew out a second envelope and handed it to Bertha. Bertha was working for Dorothy! Not Schuyler. Dorothy! Unless . . . did this mean Dorothy already knew about Juliana and me? Would *that* be in next week's paper?

————

I marched into Max's office and threw the paper on his desk.

"What's this?" he asked.

"Read. Dorothy's column. The cops want double to protect their investment."

Max quickly read and pushed the folded paper back toward me. "Give it to them."

"What? Things are really tight now. They're coming for the other half tomorrow night."

"Give it to them."

"But Max—"

"Who would you rather work for? The cops or the mob?"

"Is there a difference?"

"Not much, but some."

"So that's it? We're just going to knuckle under? We've been building this business for years. We can't just let them . . . There must be something we can do, Max."

He sat way back in his chair. "Do? Carefully. Very carefully. And I want you to have as little to do with the gritty side of this as possible."

"I want to do something. I can't just stand by and—"

"Oh, there's plenty for you to do. Give the cops their take and invite Dorothy to lunch. Politely get her to print a retraction, convince her Bertha is an unreliable source, get Dorothy to drop her."

"Oh, and I'm sure Dorothy is going to listen to me."

"Use the charm I know you have. Stay out of the rest of it. That's my department."

CHAPTER NINE

I got to Schrafft's early. I wanted to mentally prepare myself for lunch with Dorothy. She was no pushover, and I had no idea what I'd say to get her to print a retraction and also get her to not trust Bertha. The hostess led me to the table I'd reserved. Dorothy liked being seen and I wanted to accommodate her, even if it meant sitting at the largest, most central, most ostentatious table in the place. It made me feel naked, but anything for Dorothy. I nodded at the pleasant hostess in her dignified Schrafft's black dress and she left me. I stood at the table sliding off my beige gloves and dropping them into my handbag, but really my eyes were roaming about the room, discovering the others who were seated in the second-floor dining room with me. I needed to know who I'd better notice. I didn't see anyone particularly special, just a roomful of mostly women in their spring hats and flared dresses in various stages of lunching. There were a few tables with the usual man and woman combination, one table with two businessmen devouring their corned beef, and a group of kids that I knew had to be actors talking excitedly about the future they'd never have.

Since there was no one there yet that I needed to greet, I thought I'd sit and jot down some thoughts on my memo pad on how to proceed with Dorothy. I pulled out my chair, but before I could sit,

Virginia came tearing up the stairs, furiously waving. She was headed straight for me with Mercy close at her heels, trying to keep up. *No. Please not Virginia and Mercy. Not today. Not when I have to handle Dorothy.*

"Al!" Virginia shouted, all bubbles.

Some diners turned in their seats to see who she was greeting. So unlike Virginia to be that loud. She was a demur— "How delightful to see you," she went on, grabbing my shoulders and shaking me. "It's been too long. Mercy and I have been hat shopping. Can you believe it? I haven't had a new hat in ages. Mercy is good for me. Sit. We'll show you." She threw her hat box on the table and proceeded to lift the top.

"Well, uh . . ." I mumbled, still standing. I had to come up with the right words to get them to go.

"Do you mind?" Mercy asked, looking at me as she put her hand on the back of one of the chairs. How could I say, 'Yeah, a whole lot.'? We were standing at the largest table in the room with four chairs that could've fit six.

"Uh, well . . ." I sought words to get rid of them without losing their friendship.

"Look!" Virginia said, pulling her new hat from the box. "Isn't it darling?"

Virginia took off her black hat with the small brim, placed it on the table, and plunked the new one on top of her hair that was done up into a French twist. The hat was pink and round. It tilted on top of her piled-up hair, as if sliding down a steep mountain slope. "Well?" she said proudly. "What do you think?"

It wasn't her best look. "Yes," I said, trying to maintain my plastic smile.

"Uh, Virginia," Mercy said carefully. "Remember I told you that this hat should be worn when you have your hair *down?*"

"Oh, that's right. I forgot." She giggled. "I must look perfectly ridiculous." Mercy took off Virginia's hat and put it back in the box.

"Put *your* new hat on, Mercy," Virginia said. "Show Al." She turned to me. "She can wear her hat with her hair up or down."

"Virginia," Mercy said, "I think Al is expecting a guest. We should go to the downstairs dining room."

"Oh, but it's so much nicer here. You don't mind if we join you. Do you?" She pulled out a chair, sat down, and immediately tugged at the fingers of one of her gloves. "Sit, Mercy. Al's not a snob. She values her old friends, no matter how many new ones she meets. Don't you, Al?"

"Uh, yes, but you see—"

"And that is a lovely pale green suit you're wearing. Isn't it, Mercy?"

"Yes," Mercy said, "but perhaps we should—"

"Sit, Mercy," Virginia commanded.

Mercy looked over at me as she slowly melted into her chair.

"Uh, yes, yes of course." I made my smile so broad my lips hurt. I glanced over at the stairs, expecting Dorothy to pop in at any moment. Virginia tugged off her second glove. "It's just that Dorothy Kilgallen—"

"Dorothy Kilgallen!" Virginia gasped, almost falling out of her seat. "We're having lunch with Dorothy Kilgallen?"

"No, dear," Mercy said. "*Al* is. We should go." She started to rise.

"Go?" Virginia said, shocked at Mercy's suggestion. "When we can have lunch with Dorothy Kilgallen? Al would never deny us this opportunity. Would you, Al?"

"Uh . . . Well . . ."

"It's a business luncheon," Mercy said. "Isn't it, Al? Something you have to do for your work."

"I just love her column!" Virginia said before I could answer.

Mercy put a gloved hand on Virginia's arm as if she were trying to calm her. "We should go, dear. Al wants to have a private meeting with Miss Kilgallen. This is her work, you know. This is how she gets paid. You wouldn't want to interfere with that."

"I obviously know Al a lot better than you." Even though she was smiling, her tone was tinged with an undercurrent of anger. "Al doesn't mind us sitting here with Dorothy Kilgallen. Do you, Al? Mercy is such a worrywart. Tell her you don't mind us sitting here with Dorothy." She giggled and put her gloved hand to her mouth. "I just called Dorothy Kilgallen Dorothy. Do you think she'll mind?"

There was a time I would have come right out and told Virginia the truth, but she was so different now. Fragile.

"You need us to go, don't you Al?" Mercy said.

"Oh, well, uh, I don't want to be rude, but . . ."

"That's all right," Mercy said, pushing her chair away from the table. "We under—"

Dorothy Kilgallen came running up to me, her handbag hanging from her wrist, a turquoise turban on her head and her usual short white gloves on her hands. "Al, how nice you look. And who...?"

"Some friends," I said quickly.

"We were just leaving," Mercy added, rising from her seat.

"Miss Kilgallen!" Virginia stared, her mouth open. "It's really you, isn't it? I just *love* your column. Sit Mercy. It's not polite to stand while others are sitting. I read "The Voice of Broadway" every single week. I couldn't *live* without it."

"Really?" Dorothy said, pulling off her gloves and taking the seat next to mine. She wore a large ruby on her left ring finger. "That's very kind of you to say, Miss . . .?"

"Sales. Oh, but please call me Virginia. And this is my friend Mercy, and we've been out hat shopping. Would you like to see?"

"Not right now, Virginia," Mercy said.

"No? We both bought lovely hats. Oh, but Miss Killgallen, *your* hat is exquisite."

"Yes," Dorothy said. "Do you like it?" She moved her head from side to side to give us a good look, apparently enjoying the compliment.

"I bet Johnnie Ray just loves it," Virginia continued. "Did he buy you that beautiful ring?"

Instantly Dorothy's placid face melted into rage. "Whatever do you mean by that?" She threw me a look that said, "Who the hell are these women?"

"Nothing," I intervened. "She didn't anything mean anything. Did you, Virginia? Virginia and Mercy were just leaving for another engagement."

"Yes, we were," Mercy said, rising from her chair. She pulled on Virginia's elbow, trying to lift her from her seat.

"Oh? Did I say something wrong? Stop poking me Mercy. Oh! Miss Kilgallen, do tell us"—she pulled away from Mercy's gentle nudge

—"did you just come from your radio show, *Breakfast with Dorothy and Dick?*"

"Yes, as a matter of fact. It takes such a lot of energy doing that show all morning. Every morning."

"I'm sure it must, but I just love it. Don't you, Mercy? When you say, 'Good morning, sweetie' to Mr. Kollmar, and he says—Virginia lowered her voice to imitate Dorothy's husband—'Good morning, darling. It's time for Dorothy and Dick. My, my this is good orange juice,' it makes me feel like I'm sitting right there in your dining room having breakfast with you and your husband. It's so homey. Still, I don't know how you fit the radio show in with your newspaper articles and your TV show. Oh! *What's My Line?* I love it. Every Sunday at 10:00 p.m. Mercy and her friend Shirl and I sit in the library and watch it. We wouldn't miss it. Would we, Mercy?"

"We certainly enjoy it, Miss Kilgallen."

"How nice of you to—"

"Yes, it's very good," Mercy continued. "But we need to go. I'm sure you and Al have things to discuss and we must—"

"And, Miss Kilgallen, you are so smart," Virginia said. "You always guess who the mystery guest is before any of those other stars."

"I don't always get it right, but I do have a pretty good average, don't I?" Dorothy gloated.

"Yes, you do. That's because you're brilliant."

Dorothy chuckled, "Well, yes, I suppose I might be considered—"

Virginia was finding her way to Dorothy's heart through some instinctual sixth sense.

"And beautiful! You are beautiful!"

Bingo! Virginia just hit the bull's-eye right in the eye. Dorothy had no faith in her looks, but she wanted desperately to be pretty.

"Really? Do you think so?"

"Yes! Definitely!" Virginia said. "Don't you agree, Mercy?"

"Uh, yes, yes, of course. You're lovely, Miss Killgallen."

"Al, I love your friends. Why have you been keeping them such a secret?"

"Probably because she wanted to keep you all to herself," Virginia offered.

"Why don't we order drinks? I'm simply parched," Dorothy said.

I looked at Mercy and Mercy looked at me. Neither of us knew what more could be done. I would have to proceed with this audience that could ruin everything.

"A drink sounds good to me too," Virginia said. "Oh, did I tell you all? I'm in analysis."

Mercy touched Virginia's arm. "Maybe that isn't a proper topic for Shrafft's, dear."

I signaled for the waitress. Maybe if I loosened up with a drink, I'd be able to redirect our conversation onto Dorothy's retraction. Of course, how I would bring it up with Virginia and Mercy sitting there, I wasn't sure.

"Maybe we should order some lunch," I suggested.

"I've got to have a drink first," Dorothy announced.

The waitress came and took our drink orders. We followed Dorothy's lead, and all ordered old-fashioneds. Dorothy said, "I think your analysis is a perfect luncheon topic. Don't you, Al?"

"No, Dorothy, I don't."

"Give me one good reason why not. Nowadays everyone is talking about their analysis."

"This is not a cocktail party game to Virginia."

"Neither is it a cocktail party game to me. Of course, I don't go myself. I don't need to, but my friends all seem to be in it and all they do is talk, talk, talk about it. Their neuroses, their complexes, their fixations, their psycho-watchamacallits. I don't know how they manage to function in the world at all. Tell me about it, Virginia, dear." Dorothy took a silver case from her handbag and removed a Camel. She lit it with her silver cigarette lighter. Taking a puff, she looked straight at Virginia, "Now, that we've become friends—"

"Friends? We've become friends?"

"Don't you feel it? I really must hear about your analysis. As your friend."

"Dorothy, don't," I repeated.

"Shh," she said back. "I want to hear Virginia. Al, you have developed the most annoying habit of speaking for your friends. Virginia is an adult who is perfectly capable of speaking for herself. Aren't you, Virginia?"

"Of course."

"Then tell me about your analysis."

"Oh. Well. I'm not sure how to talk about it. I don't know what I should say."

"Because it's between you and your doctor," I said.

"Tell me about your doctor," Virginia said. "Do you like him?"

"Oh, yes, very much. He is very kind."

"Is he?"

"Oh, yes, I've never met a man so—"

"Let's order some food," I said. "I'm starving."

"Later," Dorothy said, waving her cigarette at me. "Does he have you on the couch?"

"On the couch?" Virginia seemed confused. "I don't think I—"

"Don't you lie on a couch with him?"

Virginia giggled. "With him? Well, he's certainly there. Oh, yes, yes, I guess you could say that. And he speaks so soothing and he makes me feel all tingly just being near him."

"Does he?" Dorothy said, showing much too much interest. "I bet he's handsome too."

"Dorothy, that's enough."

"Al, what's the matter?" Virginia turned to me. "Dorothy is just being friendly. Showing an interest in me. Why are you sounding so mean?"

"Tell me more, Virginia."

I leaned close to Dorothy and said loudly, "Max and I insist that you print a retraction of last week's news item about the Haven." The old-fashioned must have been doing its job, or I was just desperate to get her to stop picking on Virginia.

"The Haven?" Dorothy said. "I don't believe I had anything in there about—"

"I didn't see anything about the Haven," Virginia said. "I look for those things since I am part owner."

"Are you?" Dorothy said, taking a sip of her old-fashioned. "You're a part owner of the Haven?"

"Only a very small part, Dorothy," I clarified. "Our business is just fine, but those little code words you put in your column can have a real impact on us. Bertha does not make a trustworthy confident. She gave you the wrong scoop. I believe she does that a lot."

"What does Bertha have to do with anything?"

"You know. Bertha told me everything. The girl just can't keep her mouth shut."

"She can't?"

"You should hear the scandalous things she says about you. More lethal than Frank Sinatra's barbs about your chin."

"I do so have a chin!" she barked, holding back tears.

"Of course, you do. A lovely one, but Bertha just goes on and on about you in a most unpleasant way and doesn't care who she says those things to."

Dorothy lightly touched her chin.

"I guess she can't help being a sneak," I went on. "The girl's a dyke, you know, immoral to the bone. I guess that's why she lies. Just can't help herself. Sad. Very sad."

Dorothy had a look horror. "Worse than Frank Sinatra?"

"Are there problems with the Haven?" Virginia asked.

"No, of course not," I assured Virginia. "Yes, worse than Frank Sinatra."

"Then what are you talking about?" Virginia asked. "Do you know what they're talking about, Mercy?"

Mercy looked down at her lap and mumbled, "I knew we didn't belong here."

"Dorothy just made a mistake, Virginia, and this week she's going to correct it. Isn't that right, Dorothy?"

"Yes, of course."

————

"Oh, Al, she made me look foolish." Virginia knotted her handkerchief around her knuckles as she sat in a chair in the middle of my office. The tears fell. I stood facing her, my rear pressed against my desk "I never said I—I . . ." she whispered, "went to bed with him. You were there. Did I say anything like that?"

"No."

"Are you sure?"

"Are you questioning your own memory?"

"Well . . ." She got up and walked over to the window. "Lately, I get confused. I say things . . . And Dorothy couldn't have made a mistake, so *I* must have."

"No. You didn't. She led you to talk about your doctor in a certain way, but anyone who was at that table would know that wasn't what you meant. It'll blow over."

"I have to quit my analysis."

"No. Don't do that because of one of Dorothy's little barbs that most people won't be able to figure out anyway. The analysis is helping you. I think."

"How can I face him now? He'll think . . . oh, the horror of it." She hid her face in her hands.

"He probably doesn't even read her column. A man of science reading a gossip column? Come on, Virginia."

She slowly turned to face me, a small smile growing. "I never thought of that. You might be right." Then the smile came crashing down. "Oh, but my friends. They *do* read Dorothy's column. Religiously. As religiously as the society page. They call each other up to guess who the code words stand for. Oh, Al. *They'll* know it's me! I've already fallen out of favor with them because I'm living with Shirl and Mercy. They think they're low-class women."

"Well, you can tell those snobs—sorry, Virginia—that Shirl has more money than all of them put together and anyone who could find any fault with Mercy, a woman with the biggest heart in the world, should hide their faces in shame. And I bet once those busybodies read Dorothy's column, if they figure out it's you, they'll be jealous."

"Jealous of *me?*"

"Yeah! Having a secret alliance with a handsome professional man. What woman wouldn't be envious of that?"

Virginia giggled. "You make it sound so intriguing. You don't think it makes me sound cheap, like Betty Anderson?

"Who?"

"Oh, Al, you must know Betty Anderson. She's the bad girl in that bestseller, *Peyton Place*. Everybody's talking about it. It's scandalous."

"I guess I work around Max and the club too much. But no. No one will think of you as a Betty Anderson."

In the same column with Virginia, Dorothy wrote a cute bit about how well the Haven was doing. We needed that. It was a shame we had to get it at Virginia's expense, but I knew that was the trade-off. "So how are things really going with your analysis? Is it helping?"

She sat back down in the chair. "I don't know. I don't know what it's supposed to do. I talk and I talk. And he listens and he listens. He's very good at that. Sometimes I think I'm just talking a lot of nonsense, but Dr. Monroe has assured me that it isn't nonsense, it's free association. It's his pathway into my unconscious mind. I find the idea of that scary, but kind of exciting too. I do like Dr. Monroe a lot. He's handsome and dignified and . . ." She stopped and looked down at her hands. "I may really be a little in love with him. Don't tell anyone."

"I won't. Have you, uh, told him about what, uh, well, you know . . . Moose . . . What he did?"

"Heavens no! What would he think of me?"

CHAPTER TEN

I was so nervous you'd think it was me who'd be going up on that stage in a few hours. I had tossed all night. Finally, I gave up on sleep and threw my legs over the side of my bed. I reached under the lampshade to turn on the light on the end table. The city sparkled though my window as it pierced the dark on the other side of my room. I slid the drawer out of the end table and there it was. Like always. I could see it through the saran wrap. That forever to remain unsigned program. I knew that program would never be signed, but that didn't make it any less special. I had carried it with me from The Christian Ladies of Hope House to my apartment in Milligan Place to this huge place with Max on Park and Twenty-Fourth.

I picked it up and carefully peeled the saran wrap away from the front cover so I could see the listing of all the performers that had performed that night. Juliana's name was on the bottom after everyone else's. The day I got that program was the first time I met Juliana in person. Gosh, I missed her. We hardly ever got to be alone anymore, not since Paris. I ran my hand over it. I owned so many lovely things, but nothing was quite so precious as that program. My mind drifted back, back . . . I had held the program out toward her. "Did you want me to sign that," she'd asked as she passed by me in a silk robe.

Orange, I think, or was it green? I do remember she was delightfully almost naked in that room with me, and it made me shiver. "Did you want me to sign that?" she'd asked. "Yes," I'd said. The arm that held it out to her shook. "Oh, yes, please. Would you?"

"No." I think I stopped breathing about then. I wanted to run from the room for even thinking I had a right to ask her. But then she went on, with the most amazing smile on her face, flirtatious, but warm. What did I know about flirting back then, especially with a woman? She winked and something I didn't understand happened between my legs, and then she said, "I have a feeling you and I are going to know each other for a very long time. I'll sign that when we know each other better. When it will mean something." She'd predicted our whole lives like a fortune teller!

Oh, and how I had waited for that day when she would finally sign my program, when we finally knew each other well enough for that. And that day did come, her first ever opening at the Copa. She held the program in her hand and . . . and—held it and held it and stared at it and stared at it for what seemed like an unending amount of time. Then, she looked at me and sighed, "I can't." She couldn't express the deep feelings she had. Feelings were hard for her. I knew that. So, I put the program back in its saran wrap to always be safe. I would keep it forever—forever unsigned. But I knew in her heart she really had signed it.

I put the program back into its saran wrap and returned it to the drawer to be looked at another day.

I walked down the staircase to our living room. I stood looking out of the glass doors onto the patio and beyond to the sparkling lights of New York—forever awake.

Max and Scott were behind their closed bedroom door sleeping through the night. Things weren't right with them, though. A certain coldness had crept into their closeness. I noticed it from the moment Scott got home from Paris. Max was distant. I longed to be back in Paris, for Juliana and me to lie in our bed together looking out the French windows, making love and talking deep into the afternoon. I longed to not feel like every step I took was being watched. At least now I knew who'd been doing the watching. Not comforting, though, to know I had to keep Bertha around.

I made myself a brandy and soda and allowed its tingle to embrace my face. I heard the milkman outside the door jangling the bottles. A few rays of sun were trying to push themselves into the sky. I knew I should try to get some sleep before leaving for the club, but . . .

I ran back up the steps to my apartment and got dressed. When I got out of the IRT station, Swing Street was in full swing. The bright lights of the neon signs announced clubs like Jimmy Ryan's "21." The El Morocco blotted out the pale blues and yellows of a faint sunrise that was silently creeping onto the street.

I stopped a moment. I couldn't see the sun, but I knew it was there. I wished I could see it. I needed some physical assurance that somehow, we'd emerge out of all of this. But even this grand street wasn't the same. Many of the old jazz clubs were closed down. The Onyx and the Club Samoa were strip clubs now. Times were changing, all right. The club scene was changing. The country was tired from fighting two wars and now everyone was staying home raising babies and watching TV. Dan Schuyler had been right about that, but the thought of him being right about anything made me want to choke him with my bare hands. What if the show was a hit, but Schuyler still didn't leave us alone? Max said he would. Jule only had to give him his hit and it would be over. Only? He wouldn't have any need of her anymore. The contract would end and she—and I—would be free. But what if it wasn't a hit? What would Schuyler—? You worry too much, Max always tells me. I know mobsters. I can't have that thought, but . . . I don't know them as well as Max does—he never talks about things like that with me. But I *do* know them. And the ones I know, the regulars at the club, are pretty nice to me, always asking me if there is anything they can do for me. Anything they can . . . No, I will not have that thought.

I hurried to the newsstand up ahead. "Hey, Bill," I said to the guy behind the stand. I'd known Bill for years. Ever since we opened the Haven. The government only licensed newsstands to vets and the blind so there was something safe and comfortable about shooting the breeze with Bill. "Give me the usual," I told him. Bill had been a sergeant in the war, the big one, like Max.

"You bet." He piled up my newspapers. "Here ya go, Al." He tightened his tie. "So, how's the husband hunting comin'?"

"Not so hot." I took the newspapers into my arms.

"I jus' can' unders'and how no smart fella hasn't snipped ya off the vine yet." He leaned his elbow against the shelf where he had the muscle magazines and lit a Marlboro. "I think ya gotta be more encouragin'. Some guys tawk a good game, but underneat' dey're shy. Dey might be scared off by a girl who runs a nigh'club. What kinda job is dat for a sweet t'ing like yerself? Working round a bunch a lowlifes like comes 'round dis street. Its time ya found yerself a nice fella to settle down wit'. Let him get ya one dem li'l houses they got out on Long Island. You have de babies and let *him* do de work."

I usually cut Bill off long before he got to the "happy" ending, but that morning it felt rather comforting to hear him go on about such a mundane topic that really had nothing to do with me. "I'll be thirty-three in May, Bill. I think I'm getting too old to find a fella."

"Well, that's just plain nuts. A seasoned woman like yerself has lots more to offer a man than those silly beatnik rock 'n rollers. I'd marry you myself, but I think the missus might mind." He laughed, and I joined him.

It was good to be laughing with Bill.

———

Inside the Haven it was deathly quiet. The cooks and the waiters and the musicians were gone. Dim sunlight poked in through the high up windows. None of the lights were turned on yet; shadows crept across the walls. It would be hours before Lucille arrived. I usually enjoyed the quiet of the Haven after everyone was gone. Generally, I was the last to go, not the first to arrive. The quiet this morning was more quiet than usual. *I* know mobsters. I tried to squeeze out a cup of coffee from the coffee urn in Lucille's office. I poured out a thick cup of brown ooze. Oh, well, I wasn't a big fan of coffee anyway. Later, I'd have Lucille make me a cup of tea. It was good not to suspect her anymore, but I wasn't looking forward to Bertha coming through the door that afternoon. I left the ooze in the cup for Lucille to wash and went back to my office.

I didn't turn on the light. I wanted to hold onto the soft gray of morning as long as I could. I laid the papers on my desk and stared at my phone. I wanted so much to pick it up and call Juliana. But if she were managing to get any sleep at all that would be good. She had a huge night coming up. Much too early to disturb her.

Gradually, the daylight coming through my window grew stronger as I tried to focus mindlessly on the morning papers' theater and cabaret sections. Now with Schuyler in charge of Juliana's career, there were no last-minute preparations for me to do. All I had to do was worry.

Throughout the day, I came so close to picking up my office phone and . . . I couldn't. It would be best that we didn't talk in case someone was watching. This time I wouldn't even be backstage helping her breathe and bringing in cups of tea. I just hoped Schuyler wouldn't be backstage either.

———

"How's she doing?" I asked Richard through the phone. It was early afternoon.

"Good. I guess. She's hard to read today. You'll be backstage with her tonight, won't you?"

"Well, uh, I can't."

"Why? You're always there. She needs you."

"I'm, uh, going to be busy. She has you." I tried to sound cheerful.

"She won't let me back there with her. You know that. *You* have to be there. I couldn't stand it if I thought she'd be facing this audience alone. A *Broadway* audience. *Broadway* critics. After what happened last time. You'll be there. You're just kidding, aren't you?"

"I have this crazy schedule and—"

"That never stopped you before."

"I'll see what I can do."

"This night is the biggest night of her life. The biggest, Al. You, she, and I have been heading here for years. You have to be there to help her through it."

"I know. I'll, uh, yes, of course. Before she leaves for the theater remind her to breathe, but don't say it in a hysterical way. Say it as if *you're* calm. Like 'Brea—the.' Now you do it."

He tried it.

"Yes, that's right. Now, you have to do that with her before you leave the house. It loosens up her throat and lungs."

"But you'll be backstage to—"

"Of course, of course, but you start her off."

"Certainly. If that's what you want. But no one can calm her like you. You have to be there. Max won't be backstage with her, will he?"

"No. Of course not. What made you think that? Look, things are starting to hop around here. I gotta go. I'll see you tonight."

Bertha walked by my open door. I watched her go, slammed my door shut, and picked up the phone.

CHAPTER ELEVEN

*C*ar horns blared. Taxis snaked in and around shiny patent leather limos as Scott, Virginia, Max, and I—in our own rented limo—inched down Forty-Third Street, passing The Selwyn, The Lyric and George M. Cohan Theaters. Neon lights shut out the dark and announced the latest play, musical, or star, along with ads for Admiral Television, the *Hit Parade*, and Canadian Club.

Crowds of people crossed the street in front of us, making our progress slow. The driver finally squeaked past a few couples heading for the sidewalk and pulled our limo to the curb. We scrambled out of the car to join other theatergoers: men dressed in tuxedos, women in long gowns that flared around their legs, their bare shoulders covered in furs.

There was a damp April nip in the air and a slight smell of rain. I thought we might be in for an April shower before the night was out.

Before entering the Henry Miller, I looked up at the marquee. Just below the title, *Heaven is to Your Left,* blazed in pink neon: Juliana. For a moment, I felt a surge of pride; my work had put her there. Then the next moment—deflation. A poisoned sourness seeped into my stomach. *I* didn't do it. Schuyler did.

"You look lovely tonight," Scott said as he took my arm. I wore a lacy blue gown that, of course, had been chosen by Max, but it didn't make me feel "lovely." I wanted to tear it off and run screaming into the congestion of noisy traffic, which would've, of course, blocked any intention I might've had of ending it all that night. I figured I was going have to find some way to live through this, so I let Scott take my arm and we followed Virginia and Max into the theater lobby.

Virginia, as always, *did* look lovely in her kelly-green velvet gown and white fox stole with matching gloves. We waited a moment on the sidewalk. There was a bottleneck of well-dressed people all trying to get into the theater at the same time. Virginia stood beside Max, but they weren't talking.

Besides, I was choking with fear about how Juliana would do. What if she failed? What if no one laughed or they laughed in the wrong places? What if they didn't applaud? What if, instead, they whispered amongst themselves and got up and walked out before the first act was even over like they did last time? Where was Schuyler? I hoped he didn't go to her dressing room before she went on. She needed to keep her mind clear, not filled with dung. My heartbeat sped up.

Virginia smiled at me and I smiled back. Then we squeezed ourselves into the lobby of the theater. Friends, acquaintances, and business contacts instantly surrounded us. As usual, Max was posing for as many photos as he could, and it wasn't difficult. All the photographers loved him. He seemed to grow more handsome with each passing year. His almost completely gray hair speckled with black made him look distinguished and even more like Clark Gable than before. Journalists frequently sought his opinion as they did now, wanting to know what he expected from this show and from Juliana. He was appropriately diplomatic. "Well, I didn't see the show in Philly, but I've heard they've done some terrific rewrites and, of course, Juliana—I would come to the theater just to hear her sing the telephone book." He and his listeners chuckled the way strangers do when the joke isn't really funny.

Just as Scott was about to hand our tickets to the usher, Marty broke through the line. "Hey! Get to the back of the line," a few patrons called out. Others only grumbled to themselves.

"I'm just talking to my friend, not going in."

He had his arm linked with Lucille, sort of. It seemed more like he was dragging her. I thought I'd better have a talk with him soon about the proper etiquette for dating a girl. "Hey, where are you sitting?" Marty asked. "It'd be great if we could all sit together." He carried his tuxedo jacket under his arm. I straightened his crooked bow tie.

Scott looked at the tickets in his hand. "We're in Row C Center."

"Oh, that's good," Marty oozed. "We're back in Q. I guess I waited too long to get our tickets. Sorry, Lucille. You know it's sold out, so we're lucky we got tickets at all. But maybe we can get someone to switch." He turned to Lucille. "Wouldn't you like to sit closer?"

"I feel lucky to be going to this opening at all, so I don't mind sitting in Q. It's still the orchestra. Not the balcony like where I usually sit, and I got a look at what those tickets cost. Q's terrific."

"Here, put your jacket on," I said, pulling him out of line. Scott followed. I slipped his tux jacket from under his arm and started to help him in it. Then I thought . . . "Lucille, could you help Marty with this? He needs someone to dress him."

"Oh, I'm not that bad," Marty said as he accepted Lucille's help.

"Yes, you are." I grinned at him. "And keep that on for the *whole* show."

"I have to, don't I?"

"Yes!" Lucille and I answered at the same time.

"We'll see you after the show," I said to them, getting back in line.

"But maybe we could talk to someone. I'd really like to sit by you. You're such a wonderful person and friend and—"

"We'll see you after the show. We're not going to China."

"Yeah, sure, but just in case the people next to you don't show up . . ."

"Not show up for this opening?" Lucille was aghast. "*No one* would do that."

"Marty, I'll see you at Sardis," I said. "Okay?"

"What's the matter with him?" Scott whispered as he handed our tickets to the usher. "He's acting like you're his first-grade teacher who he's got a crush on.'

"I know. Strange. You think it's Hollywood? You know what they say about Californians. Too much sand." We laughed as we followed our usher down the aisle.

As we started toward our seats, Mercy came running up to us, nearly tripping on her heels. She took my hands in hers. "Oh, Al, you're so beautiful. Let me see." She twirled me around. "Who's the designer?"

"Someone Max picked out. But look at you. You're the beautiful one." She looked so much like herself in her yellow gown made of some airy material.

Scott turned to the usher. "You can go. We know where our seats are. Old friend talk."

The usher nodded and hurried back up the aisle to retrieve more patrons.

"Oh, Scott, I didn't mean to leave you out," Mercy said. "Aren't we gals terrible the way we get all silly about clothes. It must be a big bore for you."

"Oh, no. I love talking about clothes. Max and I talk about them all the time. I don't know that much about it, but Max is teaching me oodles and oodles."

"Where's Shirl?" I asked.

"Oh, she still won't come to these dress-up affairs. Not since Gladys Bentley put on a dress and got married a few years ago. You know that marriage only lasted a few months. Just long enough to sell magazines and convince the public that all a gay girl had to do to be cured was get married. And what with McCarthy and his tribe practically putting targets on our backs, she simply refuses to wear anything but pants and a suit jacket, which of course means she can't come to the theater. I'm going to leave too in a few minutes."

"Leave? But aren't you staying for the show?

"I wouldn't leave Shirl alone. I support her in this."

"But you're dressed up."

"Well, I couldn't exactly come here in a housedress."

"You mean you weren't planning to come at all? I am so sorry, Mercy. When I called, I thought you were going to be here anyway or I never would've asked you to—"

"It's nothing. I don't mind helping you, and since I couldn't get you to say you'd go backstage with her, I was glad to be there. But, Al, there's some time left; won't you go back there? She needs you. She looks really nervous."

"Where's Richard?"

"Out back chewing on his cigarettes. You know he's no good for her when she's like this. Why are you asking such a—well, forgive me, but you're asking a stupid question instead of marching into that dressing room and— Oh, well, it's not my business, but darn it, whatever happened between you two— Can't you put it aside for the most important night of her life. What do *you* think Scott?"

"I agree with you, Mercy. Al should be backstage with Juliana."

"I want to, Mercy. Really, I do, but . . . You can stay, can't you? Make sure she gets on okay and then you can watch the play."

"I can't watch the play without an escort. I feel naked now standing here talking to you with no escort nearby."

"Well, Richard could—"

"I have to go, Al. I didn't buy a ticket. *You* belong with her. Not me. Nice seeing you,

Scott. Talk some sense into Al. Oops, I forgot my purse backstage." She hurried down the aisle and out through the side door.

"Al? What are you doing? Why aren't you back there with her like always?"

"Come with me." I grabbed his thumb and tried to drag him with me.

"To a woman's dressing room? No." He pulled his hand back.

I grabbed his forearm and wrapped my arm around it. "She won't care." I gave his hand a yank; he still didn't budge.

"Well *I* care," he said. "I can't go back there."

"She'll already be dressed by now. Hurry. We don't have much time." He sighed, giving in. I pulled him down the aisle, out the side door, and into a hallway. Ron, the stage manager, was running around rounding up the chorus boys and girls who were laughing, singing, and pushing each other, alive with opening night excitement. Apple, the assistant stage manager, was checking things off a list on his clipboard as he thumbed through a rack of costumes.

"Stay out of my costumes," the wardrobe mistress yelled, giving Apple a shove.

"Ron!" I ran up to him. "Juliana?"

"Upstairs. Third door in."

I pulled Scott past the room where the washerwomen were doing the last-minute ironing and dashed up the stairs with him behind me. We jumped out of the way of a group of chorus girls running down the steps singing scales. We found the door with Juliana's name on it. No star. Yet. I hoped that would change after this night. I banged loud, frenetically, aware of the passing time.

"You go in," Scott said, pulling away from me. "I'll wait out here."

I grabbed his arm back. "No! You gotta go in with me."

"Why?" Scott whined as Mercy opened the door.

"Oh, good," I said. "You're still here." I dragged Scott inside with me.

"No, I'm not," Mercy said. "Just getting my purse. Bye."

She hurried past Scott and me.

We stepped into a tiny room with just a stove, sink, dish drainer, and a couch with holes in the fabric. A silent percolator sat on one of the burners with the grounds stuck to the bottom. In the sink there were a couple of unwashed cups, saucers, and spoons that lay near the drain.

"Jule!" I called.

"In here," she answered from an attached room. I dragged Scott past the closed door into her dressing room. She lay on the couch in her white terry cloth bathrobe. As soon as she heard me, she shot up.

"Why aren't you dressed?" I squawked.

"Oh, gosh, no. Gotta go," Scott mumbled, covering his eyes with his hand.

"You can't. I need you here." I pulled him closer to me.

"Why?" he pleaded, his back turned to Juliana.

"You didn't call," Juliana said.

"I couldn't. Why aren't you dressed? There isn't much time."

"I'm dressed. More or less. I just have to throw on the slip and my costume over it." She threw her robe off just as Scott turned and took his hand away from his eyes.

"No. Please," he called out, then took off running through the curtain into the other room.

"Scott, don't go. *Please*," I yelled, as the terror of being caught alone with her shot through my whole body.

"I won't. I'll just stand out here and keep my hands over my ears."

"Isn't he a doll?" I said to Juliana.

"Certainly is. A rag doll." She stood there, luscious in a long line bra, girdle, and nylons, so I couldn't say anything nasty back to her.

The door opened, and I just about jumped out of my skin. Probably guilt over what I was feeling as I looked at her.

"I'm back, Miss Juliana," Mrs. Bromley called. Mrs. Bromley was the Negro maid Juliana hired to help her backstage. Mrs. Bromley often helped her at home. "What's the likes of *you* doin' in a lady's boudoir?" I heard her say to Scott. "Scat. Out. Out."

I hurried out the door. "No! He has to stay here. For me. Uh, he's, he's, uh, my boyfriend and he's helping me to, to . . ."

She sniffed. "This boy ain't helpin' *you* do nothin'. That's what *I'm* here fer, and if ya thinks yer foolin' *me*, Little Miss Missy, well . . ." She looked me up and down and everything inside me went cold. "That boy ain't no boyfriend of *yers*."

She knows. She knows about me. It shows. I couldn't move.

"Now, I'm goin' in there to get that girl dressed and ready to sing on stage so's I cans earns my pay." Like an army sergeant, she headed toward the curtain. She turned back toward me. "And you can just go entertain your *boyfriend.*" She chuckled. "Boyfriend, oh yes, boyfriend." She pushed through the second door and burst into the other room.

"Uh, Mrs. Bromley," Juliana said. "Why don't you take a little time off and call your nephew. I'm sure he'd love hear from you."

"Call that lazy lout?"

I tried not to stare at Mrs. Bromley or Juliana. All I could hear running through my brain was, "That boy ain't no boyfriend of *yers*." *She knows, she knows.* I grabbed the back of a chair so I didn't fall over.

"I'm sure he'd love to hear from you," Juliana continued, "times being the way they are."

"Good fer nuttin lout," Mrs. Bromley said. "Yeah, I should give him a call. Ya think they'd let me use the backstage phone booth?"

"I can't see why not. I'm sure no one's using it now."

"I wants my same pay same as us'al."

"Of course," Juliana assured her.

Mrs. Bromley marched out of the room.

"Can I go too?" Scott pleaded.

"No!" I yelled to him."

"Juliana, she knows."

"I know."

"How?"

"I don't know." She flopped onto the settee.

"It's because I flunked Saturday afternoon charm school."

"What?"

"If I hadn't flunked Saturday afternoon charm school . . . My mother was always telling me to take tinier steps, but I wouldn't listen. She said I walked like a truck driver. My mother knew too, didn't she? That's why she didn't like me very much. She didn't know what she knew, but she knew. It's me, Jule. I'm the traitor. This mess we're in is all my fault. Mine! Mine!"

"Calm down. I go on in a few minutes and I need *you* calm." She took a few deep breaths. "It's probably because of Mrs. Bromley's grandmother."

Mrs. Bromley's grandmother? I looked behind me and whispered, "How would Mrs. Bromley's grandmother know about me? I never met her."

"No. Mrs. Bromley's grandmother was from one of the Caribbean islands. I forget which one. She taught her things. Those spooky, spirit things. That's probably how she knows. Not because of your Saturday afternoon whatever . . ."

"What are we gonna do?"

"About Mrs. Bromley? Nothing."

"But she hates me. She could tell."

"Mrs. Bromley doesn't hate you. She doesn't have time to hate you. She has family in Alabama. That nephew I told her to call tonight? His mother, Mrs. Bromley's sister, is a maid who has to walk miles to get to her employment because she can't afford a car. The family is supporting the bus boycott. Mrs. Bromley's worried her sister will get hurt—or worse—while she's walking along the road. Violence is what she hates; she has no room left to hate you. Help me get into this costume."

I pulled the heavy garment with folds of crinoline and lace into my arms, hanger and all.

"Hey! Don't touch that dress. I's right here," Mrs. Bromley said from the other room. You still here?" She must've been talking to Scott. "Scat, scat. The likes a you doesn't belong in no ladies' dressing room. Scat."

"With pleasure," Scott said.

"I's gonna he'p you wit' that." Mrs. Bromley charged into the room headfirst just as I lifted the dress off its hanger. "Don't you be touchin' that dress. That job's mines."

She hugged a hunk of dress and pulled it toward her. Together we pulled the monstrous garment into both our arms, because it was going to take two sets of arms to get this on Juliana.

"This is for a peasant?" I asked. "How could a peasant ever move to harvest the potatoes? I grew up around potato farms and used to earn extra money helping the farmers. I never would've worn *this* to do that kind of work."

"You are sure enough right 'bout that," Mrs. Bromley said, laughing. "I have fam'ly down south that works as migrants and none of them would ever wear this fool dress."

"The two of you are being too literal. This is make-believe."

"Well, that ain't no lie; it sure enough is. It's about as much make-believe as yer gonna get."

Mrs. Bromley laughed again. "So let's get ya into this contraption." She extended her arms to take it out of my arms.

"No. That's okay. I've got it Mrs. Bromley."

"And it be my job so outta my way."

We lifted the dress over Juliana's head, careful not to disturb her hair that was tied into an outrageous wig. The wig made her hair look like it was piled high on top of her head and twisted into a cone shape. I didn't know how Juliana could move with such poise without that thing knocking her off balance and landing her on her rear. I guess that was what they meant by grace under pressure. "What kind of peasant could even afford a dress like this?" I wondered out loud. Mrs. Bromley laughed as she held onto the dress. "Raise your arms, Jule, into these arm holes," I said.

"I can't see with this dress on my head. I'm suffocating. Get this thing off me or down me or I'm going to faint."

Together, Mrs. Bromley and I managed to get the dress around Jule's body.

"Mrs. Bromley," Juliana said, "could you bring me some of that special tea of yours. For my nerves."

"Sure, honey." She patted Juliana's cheek. "You rest easy. You're gonna do jes' fine."

She tootled off.

"Let me zip you up," I said as soon as Mrs. Bromley shut the door.

"You didn't call." We could see both of us in the mirror as she touched up her lipstick. "Even for the Philly opening you called. Why didn't you call? You always call."

"The phone in my office is a Dictagraph."

"Why?"

"So, I can communicate with my assistant when she's in her office and I'm in mine."

"Fancy. When did walking go out of style?"

"The thing can be used to listen in on other people's conversations."

"Really? That's terrible."

"Well, I have a privacy button that blocks people from doing that, but under our current conditions, I just didn't want to risk it. Half the time I feel like I'm being followed. I didn't even want to take a chance on a pay phone. You know what they've been saying about FBI bugging people's phones. Who knows if Schuyler has those type of connections. And today I had no time to go home, plus private homes are where the big bugging goes on. I think I caught the spy, though. The one in my office. I was going to fire her, but Max says I can't because she'll make our lives worse."

"Our lives have become rather absurd. Haven't they?"

There was a knock at the door. "Ten minutes, Miss Juliana," Apple called.

Juliana stared at me, her body stiff. "You can do this, Jule. Take my words onto that stage with you tonight. Hear me saying, 'You're magnificent.'"

She nodded.

———

"I don't know why we have to stand back here when we have excellent seats down there," Scott said.

We stood in the back of the last row of orchestra seats, leaning on the railing. "You don't have to stand here with me."

The book writer paced up and down on the rug behind us. He wore his red hair in a DA. Trying to look cool, I supposed. For his last play, the one that landed Juliana into a deep depression swearing never to set foot on the boards again, he'd had a crew cut. Maybe he was hoping the new modern style would make this new play better than the last one. He took off his thick glasses, hastily cleaned them, and put them back on again.

"I can't leave you here by yourself," Scott said. "But, you know, Marty did want our tickets and here we are wasting them."

"At intermission, he can have my seat and you can sit down there with him."

"Oh, sure. And you think Marty's going to be a cad and leave Lucille back in Q? And what will everyone in the audience think if they see two men sitting together?"

"All right, all right, your points are made."

"Just tell me why we're standing here."

"I can't sit quiet and ladylike while Juliana is up there facing . . . I just can't, but that's no reason you have to be uncomfortable."

"I'm fine. Nice view from here."

I patted his hand resting on the railing. Such a kind soul.

The lights slowly went down, and my stomach flip-flopped. The book writer behind us—what was his name again? —groaned, "I think I'm going to be sick." He ran toward the lobby, crashing into the wall a couple times. I didn't see him come back. It was too dark to look for his name in my folded program.

The orchestra began with one single note that gradually swelled into a blast of horns and percussion exploding into the air. My chest swelled as it always did at the beginning of an overture. It was like we were about to burst into the very heart and core of life, but of course, this time there was so much more at stake that my joy was dampened. The orchestra went in and out of grand and quiet moods, lilting and bold, until it rose to a flourish, and I knew the curtain was about to . . .

Slowly, the curtain parted in the center and the two pleated red-velvet sides slid to the edge of the stage, revealing small shacks with a grand house painted in the background. The lights grew brighter as chorus boys and girls in colorful peasant costumes wandered onto the stage singing. Gradually, they formed a line. I could hardly breathe. I was overwhelmed with the colors and the sounds of the voices melting into one another. Then the dancers in their own peasant costumes pirouetted over the breadth of the stage, preparing the way for Martin Van Ville. Martin, playing Juliana's would-be husband, sauntered in as the rich landowner, wearing a dark suit and a shirt with a stiff collar and a top hat on his head. As he entered, all the peasants scattered. He laughed good-naturedly and began to sing, his rich baritone filling the theater. Toward the end of the song he stopped and turned toward the wings, holding an arm out, expecting his love to appear. She didn't come out. Juliana wasn't coming out! Scott and I looked at each other in a panic. "Is this planned?" Scott whispered to me.

"I don't know," I whispered back.

"Shh," someone in the row in front of us said.

Martin called for his love again in song. Nothing.

"Come on, Juliana," I whispered. "Get out there."

The row in front of us said, "Shh."

Martin casually ambled over toward the wings singing about how he expected his love. He asked the audience in song, "Where can she be?"

Was he ad-libbing or doing the play?

He sneaked a peak behind the curtain, then ambled off stage. He came back, shrugged his shoulders. The audience laughed.

I took off my navy blue felt hat and crushed it in my fingers. I thought now it was me who was going to be sick.

Then Juliana stepped on the stage with a few delicate steps. She smiled at the audience and winked at Martin. "It must've been part of the show," Scott whispered to me.

The row in front of us said, "Shh."

"Oh, stick it in your hat!"

Martin and Juliana sang together. Juliana's spinto soprano blended perfectly with Martin's baritone. Juliana flirted with the formal character that Martin played, which wasn't that different from his real character. A few minutes later, she secretly winked at Tommie, the next-door neighbor. The audience laughed.

Before the first act curtain came down, Juliana sang a haunting solo, standing on the stage alone. It sent shivers up my arms and legs. When she finished, the audience jumped to its feet, cheering and applauding, and the show wasn't even over yet.

The second act was even better than the first and you could feel the charge running through the audience. They loved her! She got to show off her dancing in the second act. First, she and Martin did a staged version of the Viennese waltz, twirling around and around the stage. Then Martin stepped back, and Juliana danced by herself. The audience went wild.

At curtain call, the audience once again jumped to its feet for Martin and Juliana as they took their bows together. Then Martin stepped back and let Juliana stand in front by herself. She did a deep curtsy to the audience, the huge skirt forming a wide blue circle around her. The audience went mad with clapping.

"She did it!" I said out loud to no one in particular. I turned to Scott, jumping up and down. "She did it! She did it!"

"She sure did," Scott said, his voice filled with excitement.

I threw my arms around his neck and kissed him on the lips. "That should help shut up that mother of hers."

"Her mother? Is she here? I thought she'd passed on."

"Long story. Take me to Sardis, oh handsome shining knight. We have something to celebrate!"

"We sure do, madame!"

He held out his arm and escorted me out of the theater. We pushed through the crowded lobby toward the exit door, where Max and Virginia stood talking.

Max turned to me. "Well?"

"She was . . . was . . . was . . ."

"Exactly what I thought," he said, throwing his arms around me and squeezing. "Thank you, thank you."

I looked into his moist eyes. "You've waited a long time for this."

"Too long," he said.

"I didn't really do it, though. Schuyler—"

"Do you think Schuyler would've cared one fig about blackmailing her if you hadn't brought her to the level she is now? He's an ass, but he's no fool. *You* did it, kid. It was you." He took a puff of his cigarette. "Of course, *I* was the one who taught you."

"And we're free of him now. We are, Max, aren't we?"

He turned to look at Virginia, and I joined him. Together we asked, "Well?"

"Why are you both looking at me? Am I supposed to fall in love with her now just because she was brilliant tonight?"

Max laughed. "Scott, you're coming to Sardis with us, aren't you?" I thought that was a strange question to ask. Wasn't Scott Max's real date?

"I *would* like to say my congratulations to Juliana," Scott said, rather stiffly.

"And you should," Max said. "Just wait here while I get Virginia into the car." He guided Virginia through the people who still milled about in the lobby and pushed open the exit door to escort her out into the street. I hurried over to him. "Max, isn't Virginia coming?"

Virginia was already standing at the curb waiting for the car.

"She isn't much of a party person," Max said.

"Yes, but she always liked being with us. Having a drink, talking. What's happened?"

"Nothing. She's tired that's all." He stepped through the doorway into the damp air just as the car pulled up. I wondered if he'd gotten her that doctor.

Virginia wasn't coming with us, Scott wasn't really with Max. What was happening to us—my family?

"Scott," I said, "I don't mean to pry, but I care about you and I care about Max. Why are you two talking to each other as if you're strangers?"

"Maybe we are. I miss him, but . . . I don't know, Al." He pulled his overcoat over his tuxedo jacket just as Max came back through the heavy door.

"Ready?" Max asked me.

He and I walked the two blocks to Sardis side by side with Scott following behind. It seemed strange for Scott to be behind us, but truthfully there wasn't room on the skinny sidewalk for three people across to fit. And Max and Scott would never leave me to walk alone. I had no idea where Marty and Lucille had gotten to.

The street seemed even more crowded than when we had come. The theaters along Forty-Fourth were pouring out their patrons in great masses. Cabbie's beeped as they moved in short spurts while pedestrians took possession of the streets.

A group of us entered Sardis. We left our coats, hats, and things at coat check and were guided toward a backroom by Stanley, the maître d'.

The table was set for dinner. I sat next to Max and Scott near the head of the table. We blocked off the actual head for Juliana and Richard. I loved Sardis dishes with the big red S in the center and the comedy and tragedy masks on either side of it. Against the wall there was a table with all kinds of hors d'oeuvres. In the corner, a young man played cocktail piano.

Marty and Lucille pushed past the door and stood hand in hand in the front of the restaurant. "Al," Marty called loudly. He dragged Lucille across the room to where I sat. He plopped into the chair next to me leaving Lucille to pretty much fend for herself. "What a show!" he exclaimed. He almost fell into my lap, and I wondered if he'd been drinking. Drinking with Lucille? In a theater seat? That was illegal. Nah, he wouldn't do that. It didn't sound like him. "Hey, Al," he said, "thanks for those great seats. Weren't they magnificent, Lucy?"

"Oh, yes, Al," Lucille said, leaning over Marty. "I've never sat that close before in my life."

"Don't forget Scott," I said. "One of those seats was his."

"Yeah," Marty said softly without looking at Scott. "Thanks."

"You're welcome," Scott said, nodding at Marty.

"You're enjoying yourself, Scott?" Max asked.

"Yeah," Scott said, lighting a cigarette, not looking at Max.

"Al is the best friend a person could have," Marty announced to the table. "And I want to drink a toast to her. Oops. I don't have a drink yet, but once I get one I'm gonna raise a toast to you, Al."

"Uh, that's okay, Marty," I said, feeling enormously uncomfortable. "Juliana is the star. That's who we'll be toasting tonight."

"She's even modest. What a gal!" He threw his arm into the air. "Garçon! Your finest champagne for the table. On me."

"Uh, Marty," I whispered. I knew he wasn't making much in Hollywood yet. I held the wine menu on my lap and whispered, "Look."

"What?"

"The price," I whispered. "It's forty dollars!"

"For, Forty? Oh, who cares? We only live once. Or so I've heard." He raised his water glass high into the air. "And you, Al, deserve to be toasted with the best. Nothing is too good for you." He threw his arm around my neck and dragged me into his chest. "My buddy, my pal."

I pulled myself back into an upright position, smiling, trying not to look as uncomfortable as I felt. Now I knew for sure he'd been drinking. I could smell it on him and his body was flopping all over me. But why? Why would he start drinking *before* the celebration? Before we even knew how Juliana would do?

"For you anything, Al. Anything." He squeezed me close to him again.

I pulled myself away again.

The waiter started toward Marty with a bottle of Bordeaux, Chateaux La Féte. Max pulled on the waiter's sleeve, stopping him. "Arturo, we'll have that later. When the star arrives. Put it on my check."

Arturo left, taking the bottle with him. One of the other waiters came over to take the mixed drink orders. The first of the *Heaven is to Your Left* actors and crew began arriving. Tommie, in a tux like all the men, entered with his wife, Bobby, on his arm. She looked adorable in her rose-colored dress with the squared off top, her eyes looking up at

Tommie in complete adoration. Next there was the book writer, Joshua Newman—his name finally came back to me, but no one ever remembers the book writer's name after opening night anyway—and his date Sally, a seamstress from the show. The composer, Mark Hatman, and his girlfriend, Gertrude, another seamstress, came in behind Josh and Sally. Josh's date was his beard, but Mark's date I think was real.

When Harry, the director, and his wife Mabel entered, everyone applauded. They hurried over to our table. Harry and Max shook hands. "Great show," Max said.

"Anyone see any reviews yet?" Bobby wanted to know, taking a grape from the side table and popping it into her mouth.

"Much too early, dear," Tommie told her. "It'll be hours."

"I wanted to find out if you're gonna have a job in the morning so I can keep the dress."

Everyone laughed.

The conversation turned to how good the show had been and what geniuses the book writer and composer were. Josh and Mark both cheerfully agreed. Everyone doted over Tommie, and Tommie loved every minute of it. We all drank too much, but Marty drank a lot more than too much.

Time seemed to slip by without anyone except me noticing it. I kept glancing at my watch, expecting Juliana to come through the door. The show had ended before eleven, and by twelve, Juliana still hadn't arrived. We drank and talked. *Where was she?* By twelve thirty everyone began asking the same question.

"Tommie," I asked, "did you see her before you left?"

"I thought she was right behind me. She was having a talk with Schuyler."

"Schuyler?" I wasn't successful in keeping the anxiety out of my voice.

"He *is* our producer," Tommie said. "It's not unusual for the producer and the star to have a talk opening night, is it?"

"No. Of course, not." Max stepped in. "I'm sure she'll be along any minute. You know what a worrywart Al can be. Why don't we order some food so when she gets here you souses won't be under the table?"

The group laughed and agreed that getting some food was a good idea. While everyone fussed with menus and grabbing the waiter's attention, Max stood behind me and bent close to my ear. "Order me the London Broil, rare, some kind of vegetables. Whatever they've got. I'll be back."

"But what—?"

"Don't worry. You don't bump off your most valuable property." He sprinted out the door.

I ordered his steak. Nothing for myself. I couldn't eat. Where was she? What had Schuyler done to her? I looked at Marty, who was now roaring drunk and pretty much ignoring Lucille. "I love you," he slurred, laying around my shoulders. "Ya know, Al, ever since that day I saw you at City College in the middle of those cops who were knocking you around I knew I had to take care of you."

"You don't need to take care of me, Marty. Pay some attention to Lucille."

"Ol' Lucy, she's gonna be fine. I jush gotta watsh out for my pal. My pal, thash whash ya are." And he started to cry.

Scott sat sulking next to Max's empty chair near the head of the table, not talking to anyone, not drinking. He just kept lighting one cigarette off the one he'd just finished, and then lighting another one from that. Marty was still crying and hanging onto me. I wanted to go over and talk to Tommie and Bobby. They were laughing. I wanted to be around people who were laughing so I didn't worry about Juliana. I loved Marty, but I had to get away from him, to breathe. I didn't know what was wrong with him. I'd set aside some time for him during the week to find out, but until then . . .

He pulled me toward him again. "Pay attention to Lucille!" I shouted as I got up. The table stopped talking and stared at me. "Sorry," I said.

The only one at the table who didn't stop to look at me were Lucille and Apple. They were making googly eyes at each other and Apple was straight, so I figured she didn't need me worrying about her.

"Don't you love me anymore?" Marty whispered to me.

"Yeah, I do, Marty, but I need to talk to Scott. You'd better stop drinking."

"Oh, okay." And he picked up Lucille's abandoned martini and drank it down.

I sat in Max's seat and leaned close to Scott. "What is it, Scott? You look so hangdog."

He sighed. "I'm no good with big groups. *You* know that. I was thinking about going."

"Before Max gets back?"

"He won't miss me."

"Of course, he will."

"You're sweet," Scott said, crushing his Lucky into the ashtray and rising from his seat. I watched as he went over to coat check. He retrieved his overcoat and fedora and walked out the door slowly, his shoulders stooped.

"Geez, it's hot in here," Marty proclaimed, standing up. He threw off his jacket. "I can't stand this goddamn monkey suit."

"Watch your language around the ladies," Tommie admonished.

Marty whisked his cummerbund off his waist and twirled it around his head. "Freedom! Freedom!"

I jumped up and ran back to him. "Marty, sit down and—"

He flung the cummerbund across the table. Gertrude ducked so it didn't hit her in the head.

"And this damn shirt is choking the life out of me." He pulled off the tie as I grabbed him.

"No!" I shouted. "You have to go home and—".

Tommie ran around the table as Marty was unbuttoning his shirt. Tommie grabbed him.

"Hey buddy, take it easy. You don't want to get yourself arrested."

"Off! Off!" Marty squirmed out of Tommie's arms. "I gotta get this . . ." He pulled the tails of his shirt out of his pants just as Juliana, Max, and Schuyler stepped through the door.

The three stopped before they reached the table, mystified by Marty's circus routine. All eyes, except Marty's, turned toward Juliana. Marty squiggled out of Tommie's arms and tore open his shirt, buttons flying. Max hurried over to Marty and wrapped his arms around him, pinning Marty's arms against his sides. I heard him whisper firmly, "You're going home. Now."

"Which one?" Marty giggled.

"You know which one. You will not ruin this night for her. Tommie, would you get Marty a cab?"

"Sure, Max." He called to Josh and Mark, "Wanna lend a hand?"

They came running over. "I'm sorry, Max," Marty cried out, wiggling in his arms. "I didn't want to hurt *you*."

Tommie gathered up the various items of Marty's clothes and took him out of Max's arms. Josh, Mark, and Tommie walked him toward the door, his shirt and undershirt riding up, revealing his stomach and back.

"Go hail a cab," Tommie said. "Mark and I'll bring him out."

"Sure. You got any dough?" Josh asked.

"Don't you?"

"You know writers are the last to get paid."

"Okay, okay. I got it," Tommie said.

Josh ran out, while Tommie and Mark hoisted Marty into their arms. As they passed Juliana and Schuyler, Marty cried out, "Juliana you were terrific. Terra-fic! I'm sorry for this."

"Just feel better," Juliana graciously said.

"Well," Max said approaching Juliana, "our brilliant star has finally arrived." He began to clap, and we all stood and joined in.

Chapter Twelve

JUNE 1956

I ran all the way to Child's on Forty-Second, hugging my briefcase to my chest. I loved my briefcase just then. I pushed myself in and around the rush hour commuters who cluttered on my sidewalk—and that day the sidewalk was mine. They were all hurrying to catch buses and trains; I was hurrying for so much more. The crowds didn't bother me; I'd knock them out of my way if I had to. No, I would flap my arms and fly over them.

"Jule! Jule!" I shouted as I skidded into Child's. Then remembering that young ladies did not enter a room skidding and yelling, I— Oh, who cares? I jumped up and down in the center of the place, wishing I knew how to do cartwheels, so I could cartwheel over to her, skirt and all. Today was not the day to care about such things. No. Today was the greatest, bestest day of my whole entire life! Jule sat at a table near a half open window. The lacy curtain hanging from it fluttered in the May breeze. I stood at her table.

"Not so exuberant," Juliana whispered. "You never know who—"

"I can't be calm today. Not about this. Not possible. Nope. Not at all possible. Because I have right here in my briefcase, little lady, the elixir of happiness." I slid into the seat opposite her. "It is the bestest, most wonderfulest thing in this whole wide ridiculous, amazing world."

"You want something to eat?" Jule asked. "I haven't ordered yet."

"Eat? Eat? Who can eat at a moment like this?"

"Me. I've been rehearsing the new Copa show all afternoon." She signaled to the waitress. "I'm starved." She looked up at the waitress. "I'll have the spinach omelet."

"And to drink?" the waitress asked.

"A hot tea."

"A cup of tea for me too. That's all I want." The waitress nodded and left our table. "Aren't you the least bit curious about what I have in this briefcase?"

"Oh, I'm sorry, sweet—" She stopped, looking a little unnerved. We never called each other those kinds of names in public. Too much fear had ripped through our lives. "I'm just exhausted. I've been up since five with all my lessons and my exercise class and then the rehearsal and tonight it's the show. Just reciting my schedule puts me in a stupor. Don't look so downcast. I'm sure whatever is in your briefcase is just wonderful."

"It is! It is!" I put my briefcase on the table and opened it slowly to create suspense. In this briefcase I have . . ." I peered inside to tease her.

Her sleepy expression showed she wasn't interested in my growing suspense. I took out the book and laid it on the table in front of her. She read the cover aloud without picking it up. "Untitled?"

"Oh, they haven't given it a title yet. It's the libretto to a new opera they're putting up on Broadway next year. The one *you're* going to sing."

There was no way to describe the expression on Jule's face. At first, she looked confused. Her confusion turned to what might have been joy, but it was mixed with shock. Then she seemed to go inside herself and her face went blank, yet there was still an aliveness there. What other reaction could I expect when her lifelong dream was about to be fulfilled?

"But—I'm in a show," she said, too terrified to be happy. She still hadn't touched the book.

"This won't open for a year, give or take. *Heaven* will be closed by then. Look at the big hit *Peter Pan* was in '54. Still, they only kept it open for five months. They need the space for the new stuff coming in. You *will* have to audition. I'm sorry about that. I tried to get them to take you based on the work they've seen. The producers are big fans of yours, they love you in *Heaven,* but they've never heard you sing opera so . . . It's nothing for you to worry about, though. You're a shoo-in. It's got an English libretto and a New York City story line with a mystical quality similar to *The Saint of Bleecker Street.*"

"Oh, I liked that opera. Earthy. But, Al—"

"Since that was such a hit last season, they've decided to try another opera. They like that you're coming from musical theater. It makes you more accessible to the average theater goer. Better for PR. Be happy, Jule, please, be happy. You're finally going to do what you were born to do."

"But Al, these producers . . . They won't hire . . ." She looked over at the counter. There were only a few people sitting on stools with their backs to us. ". . . a queer," she whispered.

"Don't call yourself that. But probably half the people who make Broadway are that."

"The public doesn't know. If it got out about me, it would close the show, or it would never open. Not to mention what it would do to my career. No producer is going to take a chance like that."

"They won't know."

"Schuyler? Have you cleared this with him?"

"Dammit, he doesn't own you. You're doing his darn musical. That's what you signed up for. He's making piles of money off you. What more does he want?"

"Remember opening night? I came late to Sardis?"

"Yeah."

"I didn't want to upset you after such a wonderful opening, and we've both been so happy. Doing the show has made me happy. I'm in a hit on Broadway. But it is a mixed blessing."

"It's because of you it's a hit."

"Well . . . Thank you. But about the opening night party. I put it in the back of my mind; there was no reason to tell you. To make you unhappy, but . . ."

"What did he say?"

"He made it quite clear that he expected me to do his next project, and his next, and . . . You get the idea."

"He can't do that."

"Yes, he can. You know he can. He and I argued, but what was the point of going on arguing with him when he held all the cards. He reminded me he was providing me with career-building work and I should be grateful. I doubt singing opera is on his agenda for me. An opera is unlikely to bring him the kind of money—and power—he wants. The only reason I'm still 'allowed' to do the Copa is that it brings in larger audiences for *Heaven*. Good PR. Highbrow stuff, as he calls it, won't get him anywhere and, as he reminded me, 'I'm too old for that 'crap' anyway.'"

"Not for this." I pounded my fingers on the book. "I won't let him take this away from you, from us. I won't, Jule. This is *your* part."

"Don't speak so loudly. As soon as the show closes he wants me to go on the road with *Heaven*."

"No! He can't do this. I won't let him."

"Shh, you're attracting attention."

The waitress placed Juliana's omelet in front of her. "I'll be right back with your tea ladies," she said, giving me a disapproving cluck before she left.

"If he takes you over so completely, it means Schuyler will be your manager."

"I guess. I hadn't thought about that."

"Our cockamamie arrangement of Richard being your manager in name, but I'm the one . . . Schuyler knows it's been me all along."

"Well, maybe that's the answer. If there is a contract, something you signed with Richard, something written that supersedes Schuyler maybe—"

"We never signed a contract. Max told me to get one signed way back when we first started, but . . . A contract with you? I just . . . Oh, Jule. How could I have been so stupid?"

"Oh. Well, I guess that's it," she said softly, containing her disappointment. "Unless . . . There's no chance that Max might have some idea?" She put a bit of omelet in her mouth and swallowed. "Do you think he might have some plan to stop Schuyler? Has he ever said anything to you?"

Bartholomew M. Honeywell IV strutted in, whisking the door out of his way with his arm. It slammed behind him. Guaranteed to get everyone to notice that *he* had arrived. He looked as handsome as ever in his expensive three-piece suit and skinny black tie. He whisked off his fedora to reveal his blonde hair swept back off his forehead in an ivy league cut—new; a few wisps of hair fell onto his brow in a carefully planned casualness. He put a coin into the juke box and the Four Aces' "Heart and Soul" played. His eyes roamed over the tables and chairs in the center of the room. Perhaps he was looking for someone or simply wanted to be seen, or maybe he was hoping to catch the eye of that Carl Perkins look-a-like sitting alone.

I knew mobsters. This time I didn't chase away the thought. If Max wouldn't . . . —Or couldn't . . . "Schuyler is not going to take this away from you, Jule. I won't let him. I set up an audition for you. The twentieth. They'll send over the music to your place tomorrow evening. All the details are on the card inside that book. Be there. I'll take care of the rest. All you have to do is give the best damn audition you've ever given. I'll be right back. A friend of mine came in."

I moved toward Bart, slowly recalling his threat after I fired him.

"Hi there, Al." He turned toward me with a bright smile and took my one hand in his two. "Good to see you. Jeeze, I haven't seen you in a coon's age. Care to join me?"

"It's good to see you too, Bart. Uh, I wanted to ask you something."

"Always glad to lend a hand to one of my ladies. I was just going to have a cocktail at the counter. Come sit with me." With his hand pressed to the small of my back, he guided me to the counter. He tried to lift me up onto the stool, but I lightly pushed him away. "What can I get you?" he asked as he mounted his own stool.

"Uh, nothing. Juliana's waiting for me. I just had a question."

"You want to know how I got to be so good-looking." He winked at me.

"Huh? No. I mean . . ." I forced a laugh. "Oh. That was a joke? Funny."

"Your question?"

"You were friendly with Moose Mantelli, weren't you?"

"Yeah. Poor guy."

"Poor guy?"

"He got it in the head. You must've read it in the papers. Nice fella."

"Oh, yeah. Poor guy." I almost choked on the words.

"I didn't know you and Moose were friends."

"We weren't. Well, maybe—a little. I was wondering if you knew. . . other gentlemen like him. In the same profession, who . . ."

"Al, you know lots of mob guys. They're always at the club. Why are you asking me?"

"Yeah. I do. But I don't know how . . . how . . . I'd like to have a serious talk with one who can be trusted."

"I'm beginning to get your drift." He lit a Salem. "You have a job you want one of my 'friends' to do. You'd like me to set up an 'appointment'? Sure, I can arrange it."

When I heard it come out of his mouth, my breath got stuck in my lungs. *What was I asking?* Oh, God, no. I slid off the stool. "No. No. I don't want that. I just . . . Forget it. Okay?"

He swiveled on his stool and faced me. "You sure you don't want me to send someone around to your office?"

"No! Don't. Please. Just fooling. It was a joke. Ha, ha. You won't, will ya?"

"I didn't get the impression you were joking. That's not the kind of thing to joke about, you know?"

"You're right. And I've learned my lesson. I'll never do it again. But don't send anyone. *Please.*"

Bart blew out a stream of smoke. "You sure are a funny girl, but be careful. You could get yourself in serious trouble." He swiveled back around on his stool. "Hey!" He snapped his fingers at the waitress. "Give me the Child's Special, will ya?"

My heart banged like I'd swallowed twenty kettle drums. I backed up. I had to get away from him and the thought that *I* almost . . . I sat across from Juliana and drank down my hot tea that was now cold.

"This libretto," Juliana said, holding the book in her two hands. "It's beautiful. Just gorgeous. I can't wait to see the music that goes with it. Do you really think there's a way I could do this?"

CHAPTER THIRTEEN

I paced in my office the door locked, the lights off. Dark had fallen outside my window and it would be hours before anyone showed up for the ten o'clock show. Not even the waiters were out there yet. Quiet. Death surrounding me. No one must see me locked up in here. My tomb. *What had I just done?*

What if Bart sent . . . He wouldn't. He wouldn't send one of his "friends" to my office to talk about . . . About what? What? *What was I thinking?* I paced faster between my desk and the coat rack. I put my hands in my skirt pocket, took them out again.

That night . . . Virginia . . . that night . . . I heard the moaning . . . It came from the dressing room in back of the stage. I thought—a cat. I was calm going there. I didn't suspect . . . Going back there was something I'd done for years, but this time . . . I opened the door. Slowly, I think. Did some part of me expect—? No. Impossible. The room dim, only one light bulb hanging from the ceiling. Virginia's head shoved between his legs. Moose gripping her hair, pushing, pushing . . . The gun against her cheek. I froze. Dammit! I froze. I should've . . . What? What!

Don't think about it. I mustn't think about it. Not ever. Keep walking.

The coat rack shook; my coat fell to the floor. I jumped. "No!" Dark. No light. I thrust my hand onto my desk, felt for the letter opener, grabbed it. I stood ready to protect myself from the vile attacker. What vile attacker? The coatrack? And with a letter opener? I dropped the letter opener back onto my desk. The only sound, the wind rushing through the curtain. I rehung my coat and stood by the open window, feeling the damp air blow over me. I pushed aside the fluttering curtain and slid my hand against the wooden pane until it met the sill, then pulled down the shade.

Now the room was completely without light, not even a pinch of it, no street light beams.

No shadows. I quite literally couldn't see my hand before my eyes. No one would guess I was in here. No one would come in here to talk of horrible things. Horrible things that I . . . they live in me. The horrible things. They're in me. I couldn't have had the thought if those things weren't already living in me. A gun shot. I jumped, heart banging. *No. That gun didn't go off.* It was just there. He held it against her face. It never went off. It was the hacksaw, the bloody saw and the sound of cutting flesh and bone and screams and . . .

A knock at my door. I jumped, stared, frozen; stopped breathing. My heart banged against my chest. I stared at the door—locked. Quiet. I must be quiet. They mustn't suspect I'm in here. I backed up flush against the opposite wall. They pulled at the door knob. What do I do? They turned the knob left, then right. They knew I was in here. They were trying to get in. I tiptoed to my desk, felt for the letter opener. It wasn't there. *Easy, Al, don't panic.* I reached my hand into the center drawer, quiet, so quiet. My heart throbbing in my throat, I listened. Nothing. I heard nothing. They weren't trying to open the door, but they were still out there. I felt for the scissors.

A series of firm knocks. "Go away! Go away!" I shouted, holding the scissors over my head the way I'd seen Indians do in cowboy pictures.

"Are you all right?" Marty called in.

"Marty!" Breathing again, I hurried to unlock the door and—

"I saw you rush in here and . . . Why are you pointing those scissors at me?"

"I thought you were . . . Nothing." I tossed the scissors onto my desk and threw myself into his arms. "I'm so glad it's you."

"Who were you expecting? Al Capone?"

"Well . . ." I pulled myself away from him.

"Kiddo, you're shaking." He studied my hands. "What's going on?" He took me back into his arms and held my head against his chest.

"Marty, something — something so bad . . . Max'll fix it." I pulled away to pace. "He will, he will. He'll know what to do. I did something awful."

"You? Impossible. Now, tell Uncle Marty all about it." He sat in the chair next to my desk. "What awful thing do you *think* you did?"

There was something comforting about seeing him sitting there in his rumpled white shirt and too-big corduroy pants. Like me with my five or six dark jackets and skirts hanging in my closet, I pictured his closet with his own five or six "uniforms" hanging in there.

"I thought you were in Hollywood," I said. "When did you get back?"

"Last night. We finished filming. It's in the can as they say. I'm on a short R&R before I start a nationwide promotional tour with the rest of the cast. I thought they were only sending the 'stars,' but it looks like all the principles have to go. Now you're caught up with *my* life, what in the world is going on with you?"

"Oh, uh . . . It's nothing."

"Nothing? Al, you greeted me at the door with a pair of scissors pointed at my heart." "What's going on?"

"I can trust you. Can't I?"

"I'd hope so after all these years."

I sat at my desk. "I haven't told anyone, but I can't stand living with it inside me anymore and it's just gotten worse." I jumped up. "*I* made it worse and I don't know what to do. No, I can't drag you into this. Forget it. Everything's fine. What am I going to do?" A few nervous tears appeared in my eyes. Marty took his handkerchief from his pocket and wiped them away. "First, you're going to tell me what you're talking about. Then, we'll figure out what to do."

I sat in my chair with one of his hands in mine. "I'm so glad you're here. I missed you." I took a deep breath. "Juliana and I are in trouble."

"Well, you couldn't have gotten her pregnant."

"Marty, please! This is serious."

"Sorry, kiddo. What happened?"

"You can't tell anybody about this. Nobody. Swear!

"So, tell me."

"Swear first."

"You really mean that?"

"I do."

"Okay. I swear."

"You swear never to reveal what I'm going to tell you."

"Yes."

"Cross your heart."

"I cross my heart." He ran a finger over his heart. "But I've got to tell you I feel a little like we're ten, getting ready to cut each other's fingers and be blood brothers."

"Juliana's career and reputation are more at stake than mine— but I worked pretty damn hard to put her where she is today, and I don't want Max to have to fire me, so I have a lot on the line too."

"Why would Max ever fire you? You practically built the whole Haven yourself."

"I wouldn't want the world to know about Juliana and me."

"Of course not." He leaned toward me. "Why would they?"

"Uh . . ." Was I really going to say this out loud? I went to the door and checked that no one was on the other side listening. The club looked empty out there. Chills ran up my arms and legs as I faced Marty. I took in a deep breath and slowly let it seep out again. "The lead producer of Juliana's show, Dan Schuyler—he threatened to, uh, publicly expose us."

"Why would he do that? That would close down his own show."

"No. He made the threat *before* Juliana signed the contract to do *Heaven*. That's why she agreed to it. She had to. But now . . ."

"Why would he do *that*?"

"After that big flop two years ago, she refused to go on a Broadway stage ever again, but Schuyler needed her because this big investor, a secret investor, was in love with her and he wouldn't invest in Schuyler's show unless—"

"No, no. What I meant was, Schuyler is one of us so why would he—?"

"Schuyler's not gay."

"Are you sure?"

"Yes. He hates us. Why would you think he's gay?"

"I met him."

"Yeah, at Sardis. At the opening night party, I know, but . . ."

"No. I didn't talk to him at Sardis. He came in when I was being, well, carted out, if you remember."

"I do. You were pretty drunk. I'd never seen you drink like that."

"Yeah, well, anyway I met Schuyler long before Jule's opening night. At a bar last year. Before you left for Paris."

"A *gay* bar?"

"Is there any other kind?"

"For you there was supposed to be. You weren't supposed to be in a gay bar last year at all. The gray list? The FBI? You were only supposed to go to straight bars. You know what kind of chance you were taking?"

"I know. I know. But those straight bars were so boring."

"So, you're sure you met Schuyler in a gay bar?"

"Yes. Is that a problem?"

"He told me he'd been watching me for a couple years, taking notes."

"That's creepy."

"Sure is." I had to pace again. "Now, every time I go anywhere, I feel like someone could be watching me. He told me he had a witness who knew that Juliana and I were 'that way' and this witness would talk to the press."

"A lot of the press know about our kind, they have for years. Most don't like it, but they never print anything. There's a certain decorum they have to follow."

"What about Tab Hunter two years ago? Or Marlene Dietrich a few months ago?"

"Yeah, well, that was scary for all of us. But nothing came of it."

"Because they had people to cover for them. We don't. Not the top-notch producer types with millions of dollars they have in Hollywood. Would you want you and your current fling spread across their front page?"

"Heavens, no!"

"And what about that article in that new newspaper, *Tip Off*? It said gays are in charge of the theater."

"Well, that's kinda true."

"Oh, is it? And we're a cult that threatens straights into doing perverted things, or else they can't get a theater job?"

Marty laughed. "That's the kind of propaganda they always use against us, but they didn't print one single name. Because they know they can't back it up."

"I don't know about that, Marty. We live in a world that believes you must be a communist if you want equal rights for all races. Schuyler implied he could get our names in a quality mag or paper using this witness. Someone who would give an interview to somebody like Lee Mortimer at *The Daily Mirror*."

"A cheap Broadway gossip columnist."

"Who people pay attention to. Look at what Mortimer and his buddies, Cholly Knickerbocker and Westbook Pegler, did to Barney Josephson at Café Society just because he had a brother who *used* to be a communist. Barney lost both his clubs. The only place to welcome Negroes and Jews as patrons. These people have power, and the public will not come to a Broadway show with a queer in it. They could even connect Juliana and me with having a communist affiliation."

"I know." Marty sighed.

"Plus, Juliana has this Communist brother in Paris . . ."

"She does?"

"Forget I told you that. I don't want to talk about him now."

"Do you think he's Schuyler's source?"

"Jeez, I never thought of that." I whispered, "Do you really think he . . .? No. He can hardly speak English."

"Does Schuyler speak French?"

"Yes. And he goes back and forth to Paris regularly." I sat back down on my chair. "Oh, Marty, do you really think her brother . . .?"

"Could be."

"Schuyler's motivation is personal gain, but Christophe, that's

Juliana's brother, has a loftier motivation. He wants to help the working poor of France. That kind of motivation can be stronger, harder to fight. I've been going nuts trying to figure out who this person could be. I thought it had to be someone who could get into my office. That's why I jumped right away to Lucille or . . . Schuyler did say it was someone *I* worked with so . . ."

"Maybe to throw you off the trail. Lucille adores you, and I think she has a crush on Juliana. I can't see her as someone who would betray you."

"She's ambitious."

"We all are. That doesn't mean she'd sell you both down the river."

"I know. Then there's Bertha."

"Well — that one *is* odd," Marty said. "But, still . . ."

"Up until just a few minutes ago, I was convinced it was her. Kilgallen had that bit in her "Voice of Broadway" column about our club running out of money and—"

"That was about the Haven?"

"Oh, damn, I thought you knew. But, how could you? That topic's secret."

"Is it serious?"

"Please don't tell anyone. If this gets out, it'll sink us for sure."

"I already swore, remember? Have you ever considered that Bertha is working for
Kilgallen?"

"I think she is. But who is trying to undo the club and Juliana and me? I used to think it was Bertha, but I don't know. I think it's too big a job for Bertha, who doesn't seem terribly bright. But now with Christophe as a possibility. I never—"

"Bertha could be brighter than you're giving her credit for."

"Maybe. Sometimes I feel like I might go out of my mind surrounded by all this doubt and betrayal. They left a book."

"Who?"

"I don't know who, but it couldn't have been Christophe. He'd never be able to afford the price of a plane ticket to come all the way to New York to leave a book in my office. This whole thing has me at sixes and sevens. I can barely think. And today I almost hired a mob guy—"

"What?"

"A friend of Bart's. But I didn't hire him."

"What kind of book?" Marty asked.

"A book. It's about . . . Wait. I have it here."

I opened the bottom drawer of my desk and took out *Female Homosexuality.* "Someone left this as a threat. They underlined some sentences on this page, and then the first night I came back from Paris, they left a torn page from it under the paperweight. I turned to the page that had been underlined and read: "Crime is intimately . . .""

"". . . associated with female sexual inversion," Marty recited.

"You've read this?"

"*I* underlined it. Oh, gosh, Al, I'm sorry."

"*You're* his witness against me? *You* told him about Juliana and me?"

"I was drunk and upset. It was during that time I didn't have any work and you couldn't get me anything, and then you got me that job as the Easter Bunny and—"

"So, this is what you do to me? You're in cahoots with Schuyler?"

"No! Gosh, no. I haven't talked to him since that night. I never saw him again in any of the bars. That night he was probably out looking for—"

"A stooge to do his bidding and you fit the bill. Get out of here."

"Listen, Al." He moved to the very edge of his seat. "I would never be any kind of witness against you. I won't be. I wasn't right in my head when Schuyler got me in his clutches. I felt humiliated in that costume, and so when he asked me to . . . You've got to . . .""

"What? Trust you? After you snuck into my office to threaten me? You've turned Jule's and my life into a living hell. Get out of here."

"Al, be reasonable!"

"Me be reasonable? Get out before I get Eddie, our new bouncer— and he's a giant—to throw you out."

He stood up. "Sure, Al, I'll go, but you just remember that I didn't do this alone. *You* helped me a lot." He pulled open the door and walked out. His slam vibrated through my body for hours.

CHAPTER FOURTEEN

"*A*nd listen to this, Scott." We sat at a corner table in one of the smaller upstairs rooms at the Haven. It was filled with teenagers dancing to rock and roll and rockabilly, part of our new campaign to bring in more customers on weekday nights; my idea. I'd been drinking quite a lot. "This guy, this hoity-toity Frank S. Caprio, MD, says that this other doctor, Dr. Menninger, told him about the case of a lesbian who he interviewed in a state prison for women. She was there because she beat her husband to death with a hammer and left him locked in their apartment while she drove fifty miles to a bridge game. He's implying that that's how lesbians are. Am I anything like that? No! And you'll never catch Juliana taking a sledgehammer to Richard's head no matter how annoying *he* gets."

"You should lower your voice. Someone might hear you. What on earth are you reading?" I showed him the cover of *Female Homosexuality: A Psychodynamic Study of Lesbianism*. "Then it goes on to say that most of us are a bunch of drunks." I swallowed down the last of my Manhattan and signaled to Cal, our waiter, for another one. "Isn't that ridiculous?"

Scott gave me a look. "Well, right now . . ."

"I am not a drunk!"

"Maybe you should put that book away. It doesn't seem to be helping your mood any, and someone might see it."

A girl singer had moved to the mike in front of the band. She sang, "Why Do Fools Fall in Love," not as good as Frankie Lymon. The kids jumped out of their seats and started to swing, jitterbug, bop, whatever they were calling it this week. Arnie from the orchestra joined the singer with a horn solo that sold the song lots better than the singer. I had to replace her.

With a sudden rush of fear, I slammed the book shut and gripped it to my lap, my hands covering the title. I hadn't told Scott about the mess I was in. I hadn't told him I'd just lost my best buddy, Marty. I hadn't told him I was completely alone in the world — like I could be chewed up and the pieces of me spit up into the gutter and no one would notice. I hadn't told him I was afraid to leave the Haven that night. *I have to stay here all night and make Scott stay with me.* I won't be safe out there. Out there in the world. I can't go underground to the subway. That'd be like volunteering to step into my own coffin. *What if I'm followed?* What if Bart told some mobster and tonight on the subway— Cal put a refreshed drink in front of me. I drank it right down and extended the empty glass back toward him. He stared. "Al!" Scott admonished. Hesitantly, Cal took the glass.

"You're drinking too much," Scott said. "What's going on?"

"Ya know something, Scott? I haven't had a damn sidecar in almost a year. And they're . . . they're my faborite." Scott was beginning to look a little blurry.

"Then have one. I don't know much about liquor so I'm not sure how it mixes with a Manhattan, but it must be a lot better than having one drink after another of what you don't want."

"You don't understand. I can't. I can't have one of them ever again." Cal put another Manhattan in front of me. I squinted at Scott, trying to see him clearer. "Scott, you look terrible. Your eyes are bloodshot, your face is pale. You've lost weight too."

"Some," he said, his voice listless.

I suddenly felt guilty. I'd been drowning my anger by reading that book to him and drinking while he was sinking right before my eyes.

How could I be so selfish? I knew how fragile Scott was. I shook my head, trying to get it cleared up. "Tell me, Scott. What is it?"

"It's over, Al. I could feel it in Paris, but I know for sure now." He crushed his cigarette out in the ashtray that sat between us. "He's got someone new."

"No. He told you that?

"No. But . . ."

"He's never mentioned one other single person to me ever. He's just busy with the two clubs. Business isn't how it should be and he's worried. The club world is changing, and he's afraid we can't keep up. He's scared it'll be like the thirties all over again, when he lost everything."

"Did he tell you that?

"Not exactly, but I know Max. He doesn't talk about emotional things very often."

"But I know it's over with him and me. I've already moved out. This afternoon."

"What?"

"We've been staying in separate rooms since I got back from Paris."

"How is it I didn't know this? I live in the same damn apartment. That place is entirely too big."

"We didn't want to say anything to you yet. We've been trying to work it out. Sorta.

I've been moving my stuff out gradually for a couple of weeks now. While you're at the office, which is most of the time."

"That's where the signed Waterford crystal fruit bowl and the hurricane lamp went. I noticed they weren't in the dining room this morning."

"They've been out from there for weeks. I would've left one of them for you, but they were my first pieces of really nice cut glass and they match so . . ."

"No, they're yours. That's not the point. I know the two of you can work—"

"He's seeing someone else. I know it. He's always played around on the side and I didn't mind. Too much. You know, because I, well, you know, my problems in . . . well, you know. So, I understood. He always came back to me. We were affectionate. But now? He's *really* seeing someone else."

"Who?"

"He wouldn't say. It hurts him too much that this is happening. Not as much as it hurts me, but . . . Gosh, Al, I love him, but I can't get past the idea that it's wrong. This is my fault. I left him with no other choice. I just — even when I try to forget about my religion, all my mother taught me, it keeps flooding me and I can't be with him the way he needs. I know it's me, but . . . When I think of living my life without him, I just feel . . . No, it'll be okay. This is right. I'll get over it. I always used to picture myself with a family. You know, a wife, a couple of kids. I was never prepared for Max and all this other. I don't know how to be . . . what Max is." He lit another cigarette.

"I see you're still smoking. Your religion hasn't stopped you from doing that?"

"I keep telling myself I'm going to stop, but . . . It's probably good it's over."

"Did he actually say it's over?"

"No."

"Well then?"

"I know it's coming. He's just afraid to say it, and I'm afraid to hear it. He hardly ever talks to me the way he used to. About the future and the things we'll do together, or how he likes the way my eyebrows go up when I laugh, or how the vest he bought me looks so good on me. He just talks to me about business, account balances and such."

"You see? He's worried about the business."

"It's for the best, Al. We've had some unpleasant words with each other."

"All couples fight, the straights too."

"I know. But this is different. It's not like arguments we had before. There's something ugly about the things we say to each other. I put three month's rent on a cute little apartment in the village. That's where I'm going tonight."

"You mean—you're not going to be in our home anymore. You're just gonna be — gone."

"I have to do it this way. I can't say goodbye to him. I left a note."

"A note? After all you two have been to each other?"

"It's a note he's expecting. I can't have any more of those ugly words. And now, I'll get back to trying to be a family man, like I was raised to be. I'll find a nice woman and . . ."

He sucked on his cigarette so hard, I thought he might swallow it. "I have to find a new job too."

"You do? Why?" A panic gripped me. I didn't like my life being turned upside down.

"I can't keep working in the clubs, seeing him every day. That would—well, it would hurt too much. I have a few interviews lined up for bookkeeping and accountant positions in some good companies."

"You should be playing music."

"Yeah, well, music won't support a family."

"What am *I* supposed to do without you?"

Scott smiled for the first time. "I think you'll manage, and we'll get together. I'll make a nice dinner for you in my new place."

I wanted to put a foot through Max's face. Hurting this sensitive man. Then, I remembered men weren't allowed to be sensitive. How hard that must be.

"Let's try not to be so sad tonight," Scott said. "Let's dance. I need to move." He stamped out his Lucky in the ashtray, took a sip from the dribble of martini that was left in the bottom of his glass, and led me to the dance floor.

As we got up, I expected another rock and roll or rockabilly song, but the girl started singing an old song from the thirties with a slight fifties flare, "Smoke Gets in Your Eyes." We wrapped our arms around each other and held tight. We slowly moved to the haunting sounds and words. We didn't talk, we just clung to one another. Then I felt Scott's back writhing under my arms. He pushed his face into my neck. He was crying. Men don't cry. I held him close so no one would see.

———

The cab pulled up to the curb in front of my building. Charles, our doorman, hurried to open the door. Scott gave me a little push toward Charles, while he sidled out of the cab behind me. I fell into Charles's arms and held onto the red sleeves of his uniform. Things were spinning a bit, but so what. Scott's voice, distant, "Wait a minute, Charles. The cab is going to wait for me. I have a new address. But first I want to take her upstairs."

The night air was cool, and the voices were faint with a hollow, faraway sound.

"I can take her, Mr. Elkins. You shouldn't keep the cab waiting. That's gonna cost you."

I pushed away from the two of them. "I don't need you *or* him. Leabe me."

I reeled over toward the door, missed the small step, and fell onto my rear on the cement. "Now, how'd that happen?" I laughed.

I sat on the cold cement wondering what to do next. I couldn't remember how to stand up. That was very funny, and I laughed and laughed. Scott and Charles were bending over me saying words, but I wasn't quite sure what they were. *Who cares what they're talking about?* In the morning, I knew, I'd regret acting like this. Soon I'd regret all of it, but I couldn't get the regretting to come out and stop me from doing the things I'd soon be regretting.

"Come on, Al, I'll take you up." Scott grabbed my arm to lift me, but I shook him off.

"Go away. You don't belong here no more. Charles, get rid of this intruder. He don't live here no more."

"I can help her upstairs to the hallway, Mr. Elkins, and ring the bell for Mr. Harlington."

"See, nobody needs you here no more. No more. Go away. We don't need you."

Scott put some folded bills in Charles's hand. "Thanks, Charles. I'll call you tomorrow, Al."

As Scott ran to the car, I pointed a shaky finger at him yelling, "Don't you dare! I don't never ever want to talk to you ever again. Traitor!"

The cab took off and he was gone. "He's gone, Charles." I hung onto Charles's arms as I lifted myself up. I stared at the ring on his third finger. Its gold color made the whiteness of his finger look whiter, but the rest of his hand was kind of a rosy red like Santa Claus's cheeks. It made me laugh, so I laughed and laughed and embraced Charles's shoulder. "He's gone." I flicked my finger at a piece of the yellow fringe on the black epaulet he wore on his shoulder. "Jeez, that's pretty. I never noticed that before. Did you know, Charles, that everyone's a traitor? But not you. You wouldn't betray me, would you?"

"No, miss. Let me help you upstairs."

I squiggled out of Charles's grasp. "Leabe me be!" I half stumbled, half ran into the building, dashed past Horace, our night elevator operator, who sat on the stool inside the elevator reading a newspaper. I ran into the elevator and slammed myself against the back wall. "Take me up, Horace! Right up to the top. Charles is chasing me."

"What, miss?"

"Up, up!" And up we went. As I pressed my back against the wall of the elevator, my thoughts slipped and slid through my mind. The elevator door opened, and I swayed into the hallway. I stood outside our door trying to find the hole where my key was supposed to go.

"May I help, miss?"

He took my key into his hand and unlocked the door. He returned the key to me and hurried back to his elevator to answer the buzzing.

I pushed through the door to our apartment. It was dark in the living room and oh, so quiet, so quiet I could practically hear the furniture breathing. There was a slight shimmer of light coming in from the moon that shined through our French windows.

Max must be asleep in his room. Unless he was out with some hustler or new fling. Damn him! He made me so mad. He hardly ever stayed at the Mt. Olympus late on a Monday night, so he should be home. I was glad he wasn't sitting on the couch in his bathrobe reading

Variety like he usually was when I came home at this hour. I didn't want to see him. Maybe never again.

I knew I should just crawl up the stairs to my room and collapse in bed, but my insides were all ajangle. I hurt, and even the booze wasn't taking that away. Not now that I was back in our so-called home. I turned on the small end table light and threw my coat and handbag on the couch. To hell with his satin couch! I'll leave my stuff all over it if I want. I sat on it and kicked off my pumps, then slid the stockings down my legs. I headed barefoot to the breakfast nook. Maybe I'd have some tea. Have some tea and think about Juliana. She and I hadn't sat down in her living room to talk over a cup of Turkish tea since before Paris. Now, with the world watching everything we never did, maybe we'd never sit in her living room having tea again. But I had to get her that opera.

I filled the kettle, the water overspilling the spout. It got so heavy, I could barely lift it to the burner. I poured the water back out. But now, there was nothing left in the kettle. I wasn't handling this tea-making very well. I filled the kettle again and dropped it on the burner. I took off my suit jacket and threw it on the seat of one of the bar stools, missed, and it fell onto the floor. *Oh, hell, you can just stay there. I don't care.* I kicked it and sat down on the stool to wait for my tea. I found a copy of *Theatre Arts* on the counter. On the front it said, "Special Opera Edition."

I pushed it away. I couldn't stand it. Juliana and I should be at the top of all of this. We would be. I'd *make* it happen. Even if I had to talk to one of Bart's "friends." Where was that goddamn tea? I looked over at the stove. I hadn't lit the burner. I got up and slid a match out from our cast-iron match holder that hung on the wall. I saluted the American eagle on the front and struck the long wooden match against the scratch plate on the side. The match burst into flame. I stared into that flame, wondering. Wondering where the God I used to pray to went. Wondering if he had ever been real or had he always been something I only wished was real. I wished I could talk to him now, but what would I—. *Ow! Damn! Damn!* I threw the match in the sink and put my fingers under the running water. I heard a sound. I turned off the water and listened. Nothing. Then . . . There it was again. Could it be Max? I didn't want to see him. But who else could it be? It was just the two of us now. Unless a mobster had broken in and . . . How would they get way up here? Surely, Charles or Horace would stop them before . . . Unless, the bad guy paid them off. I slid out the silver drawer, afraid to breathe. It *could* be one of those guys. I lifted out a large carving knife. Another sound. I gripped the handle so hard my hand hurt. I tiptoed towards the end of the breakfast nook. I peered around the corner. I didn't see anything but darkness and the shadows of our furniture in the living room. I struggled to slow my breathing, to listen. I didn't hear anything. I crept into the living room, one careful barefoot step at a time, passing the over-stuffed chair and . . . I tripped over my goddamn shoes and fell onto our white wool rug with a thud, my hand still gripping the knife handle.

"What the hell?" a voice said.

I jumped up, the knife pointed. "Don't move."

A light snapped on.

Marty stood behind the couch gripping a bath towel around his waist, "Shit, Al! What the hell—?"

Max hurried into the living room from the dining room, tying his striped bathrobe over his naked body. "You scared me half to death. Put that knife away before you hurt someone. There are naked men in here." He jumped onto the couch and sat.

"What are you doing?" I shouted. "Max, what are you doing?"

"What the hell do you think we're doing?"

"In the dining room?"

"What business is it of yours? We heard a noise. What are you doing down here? You live upstairs. You never come down here at this hour."

"Scott loves you. And . . . and you're with this . . . this"—I pointed the knife at Marty and he backed up— "this traitor."

"Hey!" Marty said. "I told you that was an accident. I'm going, Max. I don't have to listen to this."

He swung around, and the towel came undone exposing his naked rear. "Oh, Christ," he said, running off.

"How can you do this?" I put the knife down on the coffee table.

"Don't put it there," Max squawked. "It'll scratch the finish. Put it in the kitchen."

I grabbed the knife and ran into the kitchen.

"Do what?" Max called to me.

I stood in the kitchen doorway, leaning against the sill.

"I don't see that my relationship with Scott is any of your business."

"He loves you."

"And I love him." He got up, took a bottle of sherry from the liquor cabinet, and poured. "You want some?" he asked.

"Yeah."

He put the bottle on top of the hand-knit doily coaster that sat on the coffee table and handed me my glass. "This is just temporary. He needs to think things over." He sat back down on the couch.

"Yeah? And what are you doing? Don't you know Marty was the one who put that book in my office? He was plotting with Schuyler."

"He told me all about that tonight. He also told me you talked to someone about something you had no business talking about. It was Bart, wasn't it?"

"Well, someone had to do something."

"What's that supposed to mean?"

"You know what it means. I have been waiting for months for you to do something and you've done nothing. Nothing. You won't even talk about it."

"She's in a hit Broadway show. Is that really such a terrible thing? That'll be over next year. Schuyler should be happy with his newfound prestige and his career will be—"

"He's not. He's not 'satisfied.' That's what he told Juliana on opening night. She's his security. He's going to get her to do his next musical and every one after that. She'll never be free of him."

"I was afraid of something like that."

"You were? And still you didn't do anything?"

"I hoped he had more smarts like his father, Tony. I guess not. Greed." He leaned forward, took a cigarette from the glass case on the coffee table, put it in his holder, and lit it.

"So, you see, Max? I had to do something."

"By talking to Bart and his 'friends'? That's not something you should even know about. My God, Al, you have no idea what you're saying. You're a sweet country girl from Huntington, Long Island."

"Not anymore I'm not."

"Oh? And are you prepared to take out a contract on Schuyler's life. Huh? You want to live with that on your conscience for the rest of your life? You, who feels guilty if she just crosses against the light? Is that what you want? To get a contract on Schuyler's life?"

"No! I never thought—"

"I know you never thought. That's my job in these matters."

"So, are you going to...?"

"Oh? Is that what you want *me* to do? Would that make it easier for you? If *I* had him —exterminated?"

Marty came back into the room dressed in his usual, while Max and I stared at each other. Everything inside me shook with a new realization of what we were really talking about.

"I'm going now, Max. I'll give you a call tomorrow."

Max nodded, and Marty walked out.

"I'll refill that," Max said, taking my glass out of my hand.

"I got her an opera, Max. Schuyler will never let her do it."

He poured the sherry and handed it back to me. "An opera, huh?"

CHAPTER FIFTEEN

I dragged myself to the office at the Haven the next afternoon. My head throbbed, and my whole body ached. The mere sight of food made me sick. The only thing I had in my stomach was three large glasses of tomato juice— an attempt to use Juliana's cure for next day hangover. It wasn't working. I threw up the first two before I left for the club.

I sat at my desk, trying to sort through the mound of dailies Lucille had piled up, but concentrating was difficult. So was keeping my eyes open. Slowly I let my head and eyelids droop into the pillow of newspapers on my desk. I floated through a long dark tunnel, electric sparks bursting around me. A gunshot! My eyes popped open. They *were* open, weren't they? A banging at my door. Was I asleep still? A guy stood on the other side. I could see a hat through the glass. A fedora. Who could it—? I must be sleeping. I dreamt him up.

I rose slowly, my heart pounding in my throat. I knew no one but me was in the place. Me and this guy on the other side. Lucille had left for lunch a few minutes ago, and it was too early for the waiters. My hand shook on the doorknob. I pulled and opened the door an inch. "Yes?" I said through the crack. My voice came as a whisper.

"Miss Huffman?" A kind manly voice. "I believe you sent for me."

"No, I don't think—"

"Bart Honeywell, our mutual friend?"

"Oh, uh, no, I changed—"

He pressed against the door, entering the room. He took a few long strides into my office and turned to face me. He removed his fedora and held it in his hands in front of him. "I think we got a few friends in common." He smiled pleasantly, as if there were no special meaning behind his words. We were just neighbors occupying the same world and should get to know each other.

He wore an expensive gray suit; everything hung on him perfectly, and the texture of the cloth—I could practically feel it without touching it—was of the purest quality. He was handsome, somewhere between forty and forty-five, his dark hair swept back off his brow. He looked familiar, but I couldn't place . . .

"Alan Ladd," he said with a broad grin.

"Excuse me?"

"I often remind people of Alan Ladd. You looked like you were trying to figure out how you knew me. Sorry. I'm not him."

"Oh. Of course not." The resemblance was remarkable though, and I couldn't help staring at him. It was like being in the same room with Shane.[1] I remembered little Joey at the end of the film yelling through the night air, 'Shane! Come back!' But this man was not the tough, but gentle Shane. *Careful, Al. Don't look at his face.*

"Won't you have a seat?" What was I doing offering him a seat? I wanted him out, but he seemed so nice; he couldn't possibly be what I knew he was. "So, Mr. . . .?"

"Wilferini. Samuel Wilferini. I believe you know my boy, Sammy, Junior. Scrawny kid. Doesn't know how to dress. Comes to the Haven quite a lot. Spends a lot of time with Jimmy the Crusher."

"Oh, yes, I've met him."

"Here all right?" he asked, indicating the straight-backed chair next to my desk.

"Yes. That's fine. Uh, I don't have much time, though, I'm expecting . . ." I couldn't think of anyone who would sound dangerous enough to show up at my door.

"I won't take much of your time, Miss Huffman. I wouldn't mind taking a few minutes to warn you about Jimmy the Crusher, though. He's quite taken with you."

"I thought that might be the case. He's sent me little notes, but I don't think he'd ever—"

"Don't trust him. He's got one evil heart on him. Anyone with a face like that . . . I've been trying to get my son to stop palling around with him, but you know how the young are nowadays. Think they know it all. I suggest you watch yourself around Jimmy."

"Do you have any specific things I should watch out for?"

"When Bart told me you had a need, I wanted to come right over. I love the Haven. I've been here a few times. Whenever I'm in town. You got yourself quite a club. You've done a terrific job with it."

"Well, thank you, but Mr. Max Harlington—"

"Is rarely here. He's put you at the helm of this club. You own quite a big share of the Haven, doncha? I've had my eyes on the Haven for quite some time."

"Have you?"

"And we know you've been running into a little trouble what with this new noise the kids call music nowadays. Don't you miss the good old days of Glenn Miller?"

"I liked the big bands, Mr. Wilferini, but I also find a lot to commend the rock and rollers."

"Well, I spose that's why you're in this business. Still, the word's out. The Olympus and the Haven are both struggling, just like so many of the older clubs. My boys and I would like to help you out."

"Oh, I don't think we need any help. We're doing fine. That little blurb in Kilgallen's "Voice of Broadway" was a mistake. Maybe you missed her retraction. Don't think we don't appreciate your concern because we do, but Max Harlington has everything under control." I stood. "Thanks for stopping by but—"

"Do you mind if I smoke?" he asked, remaining in his seat.

I slowly returned to my seat. "No, but I don't have much time."

"So you said." As he reached into his inside pocket to retrieve a package of Viceroys, I saw his leather shoulder holster. The handle of a small black gun stuck out. It was no accident that I saw it as he grinned at me and slapped the bottom of the cigarette pack so that one popped up. He held the pack toward me. "Miss Huffman?"

"No, thank you. I don't smoke."

"Then you don't know what you're missing. Still, I prefer a girl who doesn't smoke; more ladylike." He pulled the upraised cigarette free from the pack with his lips, his eyes still focused on me. He held the match book in his left hand and bent a single match against the scratch pad on the front of the book; he flicked it with his thumb and leaned the cigarette into the flame. I feared the whole book would go up at once, burning his hand, but he blew the flame out in time.

"*Does* Mr. Harlington have everything under control, Miss Huffman?" He sat back, blowing out a stream of smoke. "You sure about that? I heard you got a particular problem with a certain producer. I might be of some service to you in that area."

My breath quickened. Some part of me wanted to know what he had in mind? But another part was horrified. Could I just talk to him about the problem and see what he would do? Could I do that without making any kind of commitment? Not ask him to do anything? Just find out what he *might* do. Maybe it wouldn't be what Max said. Maybe he'd just threaten Schuyler, and then Schuyler would leave us alone. *Al, you're not that naïve.*

There was a knock at my door and I nearly jumped out of my skin. "Lucille! Lucille!" I ran to my door. "Come in, come in!"

"No need," Lucille said. "I just wanted—" I pulled her in.

"I'm sorry, Mr. Wilferini, but Lucille, my secretary, has something important to discuss with me. Being a man of business yourself, you understand."

He was already rising from the chair. "I do. But we're gonna talk again soon."

"Of course."

"Real soon. Both being business people, I'm sure we can help each other." He nodded at Lucille and then me. "It's been a pleasure, ladies. Good day." He stepped out the door.

"Are you all right, Al?" Lucille asked. "You look even paler than you usually do."

"Uh, I was out last night. I'm fine. What did you want?"

"I took a short lunch, so I wanted to know if you wanted me to summarize this month's *Cabaret* magazine. They have an interesting—"

"Yes. Yes, do that." I pushed Lucille out the door. I hurried to lock it; I pressed my back against the door, shaking.

couple months later, Max surprised me—or scared me—by showing up outside my office door around six. I wasn't expecting him; I hadn't spoken to him since that time in the apartment. I was on constant guard in case Mr. Wilferini came back. Max stood at my open door looking disheveled, his tie undone, no jacket, his white shirt wrinkled. "Can I come in?"

"Of course. What happened to you? You look like you've been dragged by a bus for a couple of miles."

"No, no bus. Just thoughts." He sat in the chair next to my desk. "I know you're disappointed in me. I'm sorry about that. I liked it better when you looked up to me."

"*I* looked up to you? When was that?"

"Stop. I need to hang on to at least that. Everything's falling apart, and I don't seem able to get it back on track. Things are worse than ever in both clubs. I have visions of losing everything. It's going to be the thirties all over again, only worse."

Fear grabbed me, but I didn't want Max to see it. "We're going to ride this out, Max. But we do need to switch completely into rock and roll and rockabilly. Once we have a reputation for that . . . I'm working on making contacts in that area."

"What about all our old standbys? All the singers and musicians who have stuck by us through the years. We just dump them?"

"I'll come up with something. But you know—even Frank Sinatra's having trouble getting work with this new music. The teenagers are taking over the clubs. Their parents are at home watching TV. If we're going to survive, we have to focus on the young. But we can make it, Max." "I hope" was buried in between my words, because I was plenty scared.

"Forever the optimist. I always liked that about you, Al."

"It'll be a real stretch financially, but I think it'll be worth it. I want to try to get Little Richard or Buddy Knox. They'd bring those kids in."

"Look, Al, Marty and I—"

"It's not my business."

"I want you to know that just because I see him once in a while doesn't mean I don't still care for Scott. I know how you feel about both of them. They're good friends, and I don't want to come between any of that, and I certainly don't want you to be mad at Marty just because he and I—"

"That's not the reason I'm mad at him. He told you why."

"It was an accident. Schuyler tricked him. That Schuyler has to be dealt with."

"The last time you and I spoke about Schuyler it sounded like there wasn't anything we could do. Have you got some ideas now? Something we *can* do?"

"*We* aren't going to do anything. *You* stay out of it."

"Then you *are*?"

The phone rang. "I'll let Lucille take it. I want to hear what you have to say. Have you thought of something you could—?" Lucille's line rang on my dictograph.

"See what she wants," Max directed. "It might be important."

I picked up the phone. "Yeah, Lucille?"

"Oh."

Still holding the receiver, I said to Max, "It's Juliana."

"You need to take that."

"Don't go. I'll make this short. You and I have to finish."

He sat back, crossing one leg over the other. He took his cigarette holder out of his pocket and pushed a Philip Morris into the end of it.

"Jule? I don't know if you should call me here, uh . . . What? Say that again." A chill buzzed up my spine.

I stared at Max, barely able to breathe. He was puffing on his cigarette while he read the *Journal American* that he'd slipped off my desk.

"No, of course not," I said into the phone as I continued to watch Max, trying to read what was behind his placid expression as he puffed away. "I don't know what I feel right now. Scared? Relieved? I don't know. I'll get there as soon as I can." I slowly hung up the phone and stared at it. My heart banged against my chest.

"Well?" Max asked. "Is she okay?"

I swallowed, numb. "Schuyler was killed. Shot to death."

"Oh?" Max said.

"Max you didn't . . .?"

"Al, really."

———

Juliana and I sat at a corner table at Reggio's sipping our hot cappuccinos, looking like we didn't belong. We wore spring dresses. She even wore low heels. Most of the other customers, sitting at their own iron tables in their iron seats with red cushions, were dressed in black pants and tops with berets on their heads, many smoking cigarettes in long holders like Max's. It smelled like some were smoking other things besides tobacco. It was hard to tell the men from the girls.

Juliana took a few sips of her cappuccino as if gathering courage. "Do you think . . ..Max? Not himself, but hired . . ."

"No! Gosh, no, he couldn't do that. He wouldn't. Would he?"

"We both wanted him to do *something*."

And in my brain, I remembered I kept asking him. "No," I told her. "I asked him and he said no. Well no, he didn't exactly say no, but that's what he meant. I think."

"Is that the kind of thing a person ever says 'yes' to?"

"I don't know."

"And, *you* didn't?"

"No! I don't know anybody who would do that." *Yes, I do.* I know lots of people who do things like that, but they wouldn't do that for *me.* Jimmy the Crusher might. Mr. Wilferini's handsome smiling face flashed in front of my eyes. "How could you think that *I'd* do something like that?"

"It's just that you seemed so adamant about the opera. It crossed my mind. Only for a second."

"I couldn't. Don't think that about me."

"I'm not. I'm sorry I even had a moment's thought. I'm so nervous I'm not thinking straight. It was such a shock. Who expected something like this?"

Mr. Wilferini. Handsome in his expensive suit. Offering to help me. I couldn't tell Juliana about *him.* But surely, he didn't . . . Not for me. There was no reason for him to . . . He didn't know me. The club. Oh, damn, the club. I told him we didn't need his help, but . . . Did I? Did I exchange the club for a hit? Oh, damn, do I owe him for Schuyler? The little food that I had in me started to race upward. "I've gotta use the bathroom, Jule." And I dashed over to the small wooden door in the back of the room, threw it open, and hung onto the sink. I didn't throw up. I just felt weak and sweaty. If I wasn't clear . . . Some unconscious communication? No! Never! I *was* clear. Clear as glass. Glass breaks, Al. I hobbled out of the bathroom back to Juliana.

"Are you all right?" she asked.

"Fine. I think the cappuccino wasn't quite agreeing with me." I sat back in my chair.

"I wanted to be free of him." Juliana set her cup on the saucer. "But this way? No. Not this way. I hated him so much and now this. It makes me feel a little responsible."

"No!" I said with too much force. "*You* are not responsible for any of this."

"Well, my rational side knows that. They said the body was riddled with bullets, unrecognizable. The cops had to look at his driver's license to identify him."

I took a few deep breaths, not wanting to imagine it. "Who said?"

"Harry. He called all the actors and crew himself, so we wouldn't hear of it on the news."

"That was nice of him. To do it himself. I mean directors don't usually . . . He could have left it to Ron. It seems like more a stage manager's job."

"I suppose, but I don't think something like that is on anyone's job description."

"No, of course not." I took a sip of water. "Where did they find him?"

"In the trunk of his car, uptown, in the absolute worst part of the city. The seventies. What on earth was he doing up there? Harry said it was an obvious mob hit. He was crying."

"I didn't think the two of them were that close."

"I guess it's hard to lose a colleague, close or not," Juliana said.

"I suppose so."

One of the beats in the corner stood at the table to recite a poem about the meaninglessness of existence, one banged on a bongo, and others beat on the table.

"Schuyler certainly wasn't any kind of a peach," I said, "but this..." If it was the mob no one's going to try to find the guy who did it."

"How do you know?"

"I know. Jule, I almost prayed for it."

"I think it must be a sin to pray for the demise of another person, but you did say almost."

"I couldn't do it. My whole body feels creepy talking about this. I feel like I wanted him to go away so bad that somehow my mind did something to cause—"

"Your mind didn't do this," Juliana said.

My mind went back to Mr. Wilferini, and I thought, *No, not my mind . . .*

"I have to go to the funeral," Juliana said. "The whole cast is going. It should be quite the Broadway affair. Young producer of a hit Broadway show cut down in his prime. Lots of press. They'll expect me to be there."

As I took another sip of water, I looked over at the entrance and saw Margaritte flirting with our young waiter. "Oh, no, not her. Jule, look. That's the last thing we need now. I want to be alone with you. We haven't been alone in more than six months. Just us. And you know, Max isn't coming home till late tonight. We could have my whole place and . . . you know."

"You can think of that after what just happened?"

"I need to feel close to you."

She winked. "I'll get rid of her. Politely, of course. We *are* in public."

Margaritte sashayed over to us in her silky blue dress with a scoop neck and matching wide-brimmed hat. "Well, hello, Julien," — she carefully pronounced Juliana's male French name in her overdone French accent — "and the little one." She pulled off her gloves and waved them around. "The name, the name? What is little one's name? I just can't seem to remember . . ."

"Margaritte," Juliana said. "You know perfectly well that this is my friend, Al Huffman."

"Mais oui, Al. Excuse moi. Al she is." She came around the table and kissed Juliana once on each cheek. "It has been much too long, ma cherie." She nodded at me. "You too, dear."

She kissed me from three feet away, pulled over a chair from a nearby table, and sat down. "Waiter, oh, waiter," she called, flagging the young man with her gloves.

"Margaritte, Al and I were just about—"

"You know, Julien," she threw her gloves into her purse, "I was thinking of our youth and I remembered the funniest little stories you used to tell about the girls who would chase you after your show."

"Well, we can reminisce another time, but right now . . ." Juliana's chair scraped against the floor as she pushed it away from the table. Quite a loud social cue.

"Do you still tell the girls who ask you to sign their programs that you will not . . . You'll enjoy this, Al. You used to tell them you will not sign their programs because you have a feeling you are going to get to know them better in the future and—"

"What?" I gasped, looking at Juliana.

"Margaritte, I never—!"

"Oh, you did." She giggled. "It was your best line for getting into the girls' panties."

I jumped out of my chair and hurried for the door, pushing customers who were trying to get in out of my way. I heard Margaritte saying, "What did I say?"

The last I heard of Jule before I burst out onto the sidewalk was, "Margaritte, you are a perfect ass."

I dashed down MacDougal Street, around outdoor café tables, past Jimmy the Crusher on the corner, into Washington Square Park and kept going. My most treasured memory was just a line to her. A line to get sex out of me. I was breaking inside. Our whole relationship was a joke. My whole life was a joke. I ran faster. I sped past the fountain and out the arch; I cut across Waverly and onto Fifth. I wanted to run right out of my skin. I ran harder, my pumps pounding into the pavement. I ran all the way to my apartment on Twenty-Fourth and Fourth Avenue. I charged past William, the day doorman, who I think said, "Good afternoon, miss," and into the elevator. Archibald, our only colored elevator operator, pulled the lever and up we went toward my apartment. As soon as we arrived on my floor, I dashed out of the elevator. I was about to close the door when Juliana jumped out of the second elevator and shoved the weight of her whole body against the door on the other side.

"Don't you dare shut this door on me," she shouted.

I pushed from one side, she pushed from the other. "Open this damn door!"

"No! Go away," I shouted back. "Or I'll call the cops."

She slammed her body against the door, catching me off balance, and I fell to the floor.

She burst through. I ran for the stairs that led to my upstairs apartment.

"You listen to me."

"I don't ever want to hear you again." I charged up the stairs.

She jumped on my back — "You're going to listen to me" — and we fell onto the steps with her gripping me around the shoulders.

I clawed at the kelly-green carpeting that covered the stairs, trying to get her off me. She turned me onto my back and held my arms down at my sides. "Listen!"

"No. I hate you!"

She kissed me. Her mouth went all over my lips and my face. I got my arms free and punched my fists into her shoulders. She tore open my blouse. One of the blouse buttons flew into the air.

I grabbed a handful of her hair and pulled.

"Ow! Dammit!" She pulled my bra up to my neck and ran a finger over my breasts.

"You bitch, you . . . you . . . My breathing was becoming heavy, my back arching. My hand slid from her hair. She pushed her hand past the waistband of my skirt and past my girdle into my underpants, and I wanted to tell her to go to hell, but, but . . . I was breathing too heavy and her mouth was on mine, so talking, talking was hard and . . .

"No! Yes! Yes!" I shouted as I climaxed and climaxed and relaxed into her arms.

"*Now*, maybe you'll listen to me."

"No," I whispered, because that was as loud as I could go. "I don't want, want . . ."

"Yes. I used to not sign some girls' programs. The ones I thought were cute. And yes, I told them that was because I had a feeling we were going to get to know to each other better in the future and if I signed it later, it would mean more. And yes, it was a line. But Al, you're smart. How could you have thought I could predict such a thing between you and me?"

"You looked wise. So, what? You shouldn't have done it. Don't blame me. I thought that was an important moment between us. I still have that program preserved in my end table drawer?"

"That's sweet and so you."

"Oh, yeah, sure."

"It is. But I had no way of knowing, then, that you would be different from the others. That you'd be still hanging around all these many years later."

"Sorry I'm such an annoyance, but you don't have to worry. I won't be 'hanging around' anymore." I tried to get up, but she held me down.

"I kept wondering when you were going to leave me like the rest. Why you hadn't taken off a long time ago. I haven't used that 'line' in years. I couldn't use it anymore."

"Because of me?"

"Well . . ."

"Yeah. Because of me, and you know what, Jule?"

"What?"

"You chased after your woman today."

"You little brat." She tried to turn me over and spank me, but I jumped up and ran behind the piano. "You've chased after me a whole lot over the years."

She ran after me, grabbed me — I didn't put up much of a fight — and pulled me over her lap as she sat on the couch. She pulled up my dress and slid off my underpants and gave me a few hard whacks to my rear end.

We laughed and rolled off the couch onto Max's spotless white rug. We made love to each other and then lay on our backs holding hands. Our clothes were all in disarray, our blouses spread open, our girdles, stockings, underpants somewhere in the room.

"You know what let's do?" Juliana said as we both lay in the middle of the rug. "Let's go away together. Just the two of us. Richard and I have this cabin up in the mountains in Maine. Let's go there next Sunday. The theater is dark, so we'll have the whole day and night. As long as I get back here for the Monday night show, everything will be fine."

"Won't Richard mind?"

"Very much. But we won't tell him, will we? He hasn't been to the cabin in years. I've used it myself from time to time to get a little respite from the city. Richard has hay fever, so all that green foliage gets to him."

"It's green? It has trees and grass and fresh air?"

She leaned on one elbow, looking down at me. "Yes, it does, and a lake."

"A lake? For swimming?"

"Uh, huh. You'd like that, wouldn't you?"

"I haven't been around green living breathing things without honking traffic in seventeen years. Ever since I came here. I would love that." I sat up. "We can really do this, Jule? Just you and me? But what if someone sees us? Even with Schuyler, uh, well . . . these days you never know who might be spying."

"I'll fly up early Sunday morning right after six o'clock mass and get things ready. Air it out, clean. No one's been there in a couple years, so it'll need it. You follow in a later plane, mid-morning. You can get a cab at the airport to bring you over. Give him an especially large tip, just in case. Have him leave you off at the cabin. I won't come out, so he doesn't see me. You have to come in to let me know the coast is clear."

"Such intrigue."

"Once you're there, we'll be safe. We won't have a lot of time, but it's something."

"You're serious? We're really going to do this, Jule? Be alone together in a mountain retreat? That's really going to happen?"

"That's really going to happen."

CHAPTER SEVENTEEN

*M*ax and I stepped into the sanctuary of Holy Cross Roman Catholic Church in Times Square. We followed a line of people silently entering and sliding into the dark brown maple wood pews, their heads bowed. Behind and above us, men in black choir robes stood in the balcony singing Gregorian chants that filled the room with vibrating holiness. Our line crept slowly up the aisle; women and men genuflected to the huge gold crucifix hanging above the altar. Across from us beyond the central pews was another aisle with its own line of silently entering people. Max crossed himself.

"Max, you're Catholic?" I whispered.

"On my mother's side. Very lapsed. Let's go in here."

We slid into a pew and sat a moment with our heads bowed. *He* was up there. Schuyler. Inside that shut up mahogany coffin. Strangely, it reminded me of the hope chest I had as a girl. Except my hope chest was made of cedar to make the linens inside smell good. Hope chest—coffin. Kind of the same thing. Surrounding the coffin were six white tapering candles, aflame. They sat in real gold floor-length candlesticks. On the altar were some smaller candles, a crucifix, and a book propped up by a stand.

I wondered where Juliana was. The place was packed. All of

Broadway had shown up for Schuyler's funeral. You would've thought he was popular, but *Heaven is to Your Left* was only his first production. Still, he *was* the lead producer of a giant hit. People like to cozy up to that. Except — he was dead. What good could he do for them now? This show had been put together by his estranged wife. At least that's what I heard. They never divorced like he told me on the ship. Catholic. They just separated. I guess because they couldn't stand each other. Who could stand living with a guy like Schuyler. Still, it was big of her to plan the funeral of a man she detested. Or did she? I craned my neck trying to get a glimpse of Juliana. I saw Martin Van Ville sitting close to the front, his head bowed, a yarmulke on his head. I didn't know he was Jewish. I couldn't see anyone else from the cast.

I swirled around to look at the people still entering. The line snaked onto the sidewalk beyond the open church door. *He was that popular?*

The minister, uh, priest in his black robes stepped up to the altar and the hum of faint voices ceased. His two helpers stood on either side of him, also in black robes. The priest faced the altar, which meant he had his back to us. Then he sang. He sang what I supposed was a Latin song.

It sure was a long service, I mean mass. Everything was in Latin, so I didn't know why we were doing what we were doing, but I followed along. First, we stood, then we sat, then we kneeled, then we stood, then we sat, then we kneeled. Up down, up down. It was making me dizzy. Then the collection plate came around. At home, in my little starving church, if the minister passed the collection plate at a funeral, everyone would've gotten up, told him off and probably the next day he would've found himself fired.

After they collected the money, and everyone said a prayer together in Latin—a lot of people seemed to know this prayer—one of the helpers announced it was time for Holy Communion. That's another thing we didn't do in our church at a funeral. It takes too long. I think maybe protestants at a funeral are in a hurry to finish church so they can go to the reception to eat. They don't want to bother with extra stuff like communion. The priest talked to us from the altar. This time he faced us. He made it very clear that, even though he loved us, people like me did not qualify to take communion in *his* church; we'd better not crash their Catholic ceremony or something terrible would fall on our heads. Max and I just sat back watching all the people who did qualify go up to the altar and kneel with their tongues out. That's when I saw Juliana and Richard. They were approaching the altar. Juliana looked pretty in a navy blue suit with white trim on the sleeves and collar. Her navy, blue hat had a white trim too that ran around the edges. She looked respectful without seeming dead the way all the people who wore black like me did. Did Schuyler deserve me dressing in black like I was all broken up about him? Wasn't it phony? Weren't we all being phonies like Holden Caulfield says in *Catcher in the Rye*, that book that came out a few years ago. A real good book. At home one time we had a minister who came to a funeral in a red jacket. Boy, did the old biddies in my church waste no time getting rid of him. But if going to heaven is supposed be a really great thing, why *wouldn't* you wear red and be all happy that the person is dead? I couldn't let myself be happy about Schuyler, but I decided I didn't do anything to rush him on his way.

Holy Communion took a long time. Max kept falling asleep in his pew and I had to elbow him awake. After a while, I found myself watching the communion folks more closely. Some of them really did look holy when they left the altar, their heads bowed, their hands crossed over their chest or in prayer position. They looked like something had truly happened to them. Inwardly. One old woman even cried. Juliana looked peaceful, as if holding the wafer on her tongue had made her safe inside.

When everyone was back in their seats, the two assistants came down the aisles shaking incense at us. A powerful purple smell. The service—uh, mass—ended, and we were instructed to file out in silence so the family could be alone with the body. Gosh, I'd hate to be called 'the body'— but I guess that's what I'll be someday. Everything seemed so holy, especially as we were walking out in silence. How could there be this much holiness for a man like Schuyler? He wasn't a good man. How could he be good and still force Juliana into his play? Which was a huge hit, making Juliana's name known around the country. *That's not a bad thing, Al.*

Yes, but . . .

"Ready, Al?" Max said when we got to the church's front steps.

I wasn't sure why Max decided to join the funeral procession and go to the burial. It made me wonder again if Max had something to do with— No, he didn't. He said he didn't. Didn't he? Yes. Forget it. Maybe we were going because we both wanted to be sure they put him in the ground, that he was gone, really gone. For good.

We crossed the street where he'd parked our Continental Mark II rental with the fancy metal logo on the hood—a four-pointed star inside a rectangle. Only the best for Max, no matter what our account books said. As Max came around the car to the passenger side to open the door for me, I saw the pall bearers pushing the coffin into the back of the hearse. I froze a moment. *I had nothing to do with that. Did I?*

"You all right, Al?" Max asked, standing next to the car door he'd just opened. "You're not thinking bad thoughts, are you?"

"Bad thoughts? Never. Only good ones."

"Good."

I got into the car and he closed the door. He ran around to the driver's side. I wondered why he asked me about my thoughts. What'd he mean by bad thoughts? Were these bad thoughts I *should* have or ones he didn't want me to have? Was he the one having bad thoughts? About himself, or me? Did he know I met with Mr. Wilferini? Did he suspect that I . . .?

With our headlights on, we followed the line of cars toward the graveyard. It would take a while since it was in Brooklyn. It started to sprinkle, so Max put on the wipers. "Open that envelope on the seat. It's for you."

I picked it up. The front was blank.

"It's from Marty," he said.

"Come on, Max. Stay out of it." I put the envelope back on the seat between us.

"Read it."

"Why? Did you write it?"

"No. He wrote it himself. It's from his heart. He's really upset about everything."

"Why didn't he mail it instead of getting my 'boss' involved?"

"Your boss? My goodness. He finished it at the airport and asked me to give it to you. He was rushing to catch a plane back to Hollywood."

My hand inched over toward the letter and touched it. "You know, Max, living in the world we live in—"

"What world is that?"

"Stop. You know. The world where one false move can get you destroyed in one way or another. You have to be able to trust your friends. So, he gets mad at me and betrays me to some guy he just met in a bar—Schuyler."

"He thought he was gay."

"What difference does that make?" My anger was beginning to boil up again. "He put that poisonous book on my desk knowing it would upset me, knowing it would scare me. And you and I both know there are those of our own kind who would squawk like canaries if it meant a few extra bucks or a part in a show. Look what that gay boy press agent, whatever his name was, did to his Fire Island buddies a few years ago."

"Oh, yeah, he got Dorothy to write that bit about them in her column. She loved that. A bunch of matinee idols. I suppose anyone who knew how to decipher Kilgallen's code could have caused them real trouble. They could have lost some fans, but—"

"Or jobs. Like some did. Or careers. That code wasn't so hard to decipher." I recited, "The newspapers will never print the real story behind the recent show business marriage crash. It was *Well of Loneliness* time."

"You memorized it?"

"I had to. I'm looking out for my survival."

"That's very odd, Al. Open Marty's letter."

I took the envelope into my hand. I missed him. I missed him being my friend. I loved him. But how would I ever trust him again?

Max swerved the car so he could get around the Chevy that was trying to break through our funeral procession. The sprinkle had turned into a steadier drizzle, rhythmically hitting the windshield before it was whisked away by the wipers. I gripped the envelope with my hands, practically crushing it.

"You know what he got me for *his* going away?' Max asks. "A transistor radio."

"No kidding? Does that thing really work? Can you really walk outside the apartment into the street and it still plays? No plug?"

"No plug. You use this strange new battery, a nine-volt, that seems to take the place of the plug. As long as the antenna can catch the radio waves, you can listen to it wherever you are. I'll show you when we get back. It's small so it's easy to carry around. But do you know what one of those things cost?"

"I stopped in a TV/Radio store once because I was curious. I've been seeing a lot of kids with them listening to their rock and roll, so I figured I'd better find out what's going on. The ones I looked at were fifty dollars!"

Max nodded. "Uh, huh. I tell him he's got to save his money; this business is fickle, and producers can turn on you in a second. He won't listen. He's not wise about money."

I ran my hand over the soft leather interior from Scotland and gave Max a look. "I wonder where he got that from?"

"Not me. This is a rental."

"A very expensive rental."

"Well, we can't exactly show up at *this* funeral with all the hoity-toitiest people in town in a borrowed pickup truck, can we? We're not talking about me. We're talking about Marty. There are times when he can be downright foolish, but he has a lot of love. And I know you're very special to him. When he and I first started dating, all he kept talking about was you and how he didn't want to hurt your friend Scott because he knew it would hurt you. He told me he couldn't stand it that you were mad at him."

I pulled the envelope open. Max lit a Chesterfield with the car lighter and slid open the ashtray. I slipped out the folded white paper and stared through the side window, watching the rain come down in sheets. I was afraid I wouldn't like what he said in the letter and I'd have to permanently expel him from my life. I didn't want to do that.

My mind drifted back to another time. My first year of school, forty-eight. I was excited and scared. What was I doing at a college? That was about as far as I had ever imagined myself being. My family thought I might work in an orchard picking oranges until I got married. Or, perhaps in a factory sticking some part to another part. They never planned on me going to New York City and they certainly never planned on college, but there I was. It was spring. I had begun my classes and I'd heard rumors of a protest march or a sit-down strike or one of those. I wasn't sure what it was about, but I wanted to be a part of whatever was happening at school. I joined a line of students, held my sign high, and marched with them. "Jim Crow Must Go!" Suddenly cops and paddy wagons were everywhere, and kids were running and I was running and kids were being knocked down all around me; some were hit with clubs. I ran as fast as I could. A slam to my head. I almost went down when someone grabbed my arm and ran with me. We ran out the gates and down the street. We didn't stop till we got to a telephone pole near the subway entrance. Then I saw—it was Marty. His dark hair falling over his brow, no tie or jacket, his corduroy pants too big for him. He had saved me from that mob. I could've been trampled.

I unfolded the letter on my lap, smoothing out the creases. "Hi Al, I'm headed back to LA again. Sorry there was no time to talk in person before I left. I'm hoping Max will give this to you."

It felt like he was right in the car with me, sitting in the center between Max and me.

"I hurt you. I know I hurt you bad and there may not be anything I can ever do to fix that. But I want to fix it. I want to fix it so desperately. I was drunk when I took that book from Schuyler and put it in your office. I know that isn't an excuse. But I was so drunk I forgot I left it there. If I hadn't forgotten, I would've gone back and gotten it off your desk when I sobered up. Then you wouldn't have seen it and none of this between us would've happened. As I sit here writing and watching the sun rise over the airplanes, I feel so ashamed. It isn't the me I know who goes around hurting special people, but I did it. It's hard for me to believe, but I did do it. And I am so, so sorry. I understand if you never talk to me again or never trust me again, but I'm going to spend the rest of my life trying to make it up to you. I also wanted to tell you that I didn't break up Max and Scott. I just happened to be around when they were already breaking up. That's what Max told me, so you can ask him.

"You are so special to me and I lost touch with that until I lost you. I want you back. Please. What do I have to do? Anything? Anything.

Please forgive me. Your friend, *Marty*

P.S. A little something to cheer you up. Katharine Hepburn likes girls."

I laughed.

"Funny?" Max asked.

I folded the letter back into its envelope. "Not really."

We turned into a wide drive and stopped. In front of us was a line of cars with their lights on and a huge brown stone gate with spires that pierced the clouds above us. In the center of the spires, a bell tower. On either side of the bell tower and spires were house-like structures made of the same brown stone. As we slowly drove toward the structure, my breath caught in my lungs with the massiveness of it. And the thought that a sculptor had created this for the dead. Or maybe he did it for the people who came to bury the dead. To uplift them in their sorrow. Max steered us under the bell tower and out onto a tree-lined road. The grass on either side was greener than I'd seen grass in a long time. Actually, I hardly ever saw grass anymore, so I enjoyed filling my eyes with all that green.

As we crept along the road, the rain hitting the windshield with more force, I was swept back to another time. A springtime when I was a child and sat in our backyard by the old maple, devouring classic literature. "Oh, Max," I said with a joy bursting out of me, "look at these trees. I've never seen trees this fat with leaves in my life. And those tree trunks thick and twisted into bizarre sculptured shapes."

"Look up ahead," Max said. "It's like a museum. Some of the graves have the most the incredible marble sculptures on top. Too grand for Schuyler."

"But it doesn't look Catholic. I haven't seen one crucifix or Madonna sculpture."

"I doubt you will. It's kind of a nondenominational cemetery, so mostly protestants are buried here."

"But Schuyler's Catholic."

"I heard the priest was a buddy of Schuyler's wife, or maybe her paramour."

"What?"

"Well, they were separated, but you better still keep that to yourself. Not good for the priest. He did the service for her as a favor. I gather Schuyler wasn't a very good Catholic."

"He wasn't a very good anything."

"He was good enough for the priest to pull off that elaborate high mass, but evidently not good enough to convince the powers that be to let him be buried in consecrated grounds. Personally, I think it's better here. I wouldn't mind being buried here."

Max followed the other cars around a curve and pulled onto the side of the road near a grassy hill. He got out and ran around the car with an open umbrella for me. He opened my door and held the umbrella over my head while he got soaked crossing us both to the other side of the road. When I tried to share the umbrella with him, he insisted he needed to remain a gentleman for the sake of his dignity. So, he continued to get rained on. Didn't really seem fair. We walked over to the small crowd that had gathered under a tarp mounted on poles and held in place with ropes and stakes pounded into the ground. The crowd was much smaller than the one at the church. The coffin had been placed in a partially dug hole with loose dirt surrounding it. It was nice-looking dirt. Clean, if you could ever call dirt clean, with a rich darkness to it. Loose and fluffy. I had an urge to run my hands through it. I resisted.

We walked under the tarp and took seats on the folding chairs that had been placed around the coffin. Juliana and Richard sat in the row opposite us, their heads bowed. Martin VanVille, Harry Fielding, and Ron Stein, our stage manager, also sat on the opposite side.

The priest, his hands folded over a Bible, approached the coffin. "We are gathered here today to mourn the passing of the beloved husband of Martha Wine Schuyler." If she thought he was so damn "beloved," why had they been separated for four years? Why was she having an affair with a priest? But that was a rumor. Maybe she wasn't. "And the father of Daniel Schuyler,

Jr. Before proceeding, Martha, young Daniel and a good friend of the senior Daniel desire to speak."

Schuyler had friends?

Martha Wine Schuyler was sitting on the end of my row next to the young man I suspected was her son. She stood and approached the coffin. She was a rather large woman, not fat, but big-shouldered and bosomed. She looked much sturdier than the willowy Schuyler and older, more like his mother. She wore a flower-print dress with a large purple hat. Flowery material at a funeral and a purple hat? That must be a hint of how she truly felt. She cleared her throat and intertwined her lacy handkerchief through her stubby fingers. "My husband, Daniel, was a good man," she began. "A good and decent man. Kind to all he met. A philanthropist even when he had little of his own to give. Struck down too soon."

Too soon? Was she expecting it, but at some later date? It felt strange to be at the funeral of someone who had so obviously been murdered. But everyone seemed to be ignoring that little detail. She wiped away her tears with her handkerchief. *Was she telling the truth?* How could he have been so wonderful to her and so horrible to us? She was lying. She had to lie so people wouldn't wonder why she'd married such a creep, or why she'd put together this beautiful funeral. Or if she really was dating a priest? No woman would date a priest. That's ridiculous. Still, she had to make him look good or she'd seem like a fool. But — they were separated, so why did she have to say *anything*? Why did she have to lie? Was she involved with his murder?

"By the large number of people who came to the church today and you special people who have come to the grave," she continued, "it is apparent that Daniel shall be sorely missed by many. God works in mysterious ways, and he has seen fit to take Daniel from the beloved womb of his family and friends. Daniel now lives among the angels."

An angel? What pictures had she been going to? This was more like a canned speech from a minister who didn't know him. Rain beat rhythmically against the canvas over our heads.

Dan Schuyler, Jr.—tall, thin, about twenty-one—stood as his mother sat down. Dan Sr. must have been older than he looked or else he got married and had Dan Jr. as a teenager. Dan Jr. looked freakishly like the man, Dan Sr. Only he was even lankier and seemed unstable on his feet. As he scrambled to take his place near the coffin, my eyes wandered over toward the lake not far from us. Scattered around it were individual mausoleums, looking like beach houses with a good view of the water. Only the occupants of these houses were dead. What difference could a good view possibly make to people in their condition?

When Dan Jr. spoke, I nearly jumped out of my skin, his voice sounded so much like his father's. It was like listening to a ghost. I grabbed Max's hand as the young man extolled his father's virtues. "The best dad a guy could have." He told a story about how he'd been afraid to ride his bike without training wheels when he was small, and his father had gently helped him to confront his fear. My stomach turned into one knotted ball as I pictured Schuyler bending over his child, kissing his head. Later there had been money problems in the family. Schuyler couldn't afford to send his son to an Ivy League college like the rest of the fathers in the boy's class. The last of his savings had gone to help Dan Sr.'s father, Tony, the Broadway producer, who was dying of cancer.

What? Tony was the producer Shirl knew. She said Tony went broke paying out money to keep Dan out of trouble, not the other way around. She said Tony died penniless, every cent gone trying to find Dan Sr., who had disappeared before Tony died. Shirl wouldn't have lied or made something up. Could she have gotten the story wrong? No. Look how he treated Juliana and me in Paris. Look how he acted in that makeshift office when I went to see him in Pegalle. That was the real Schuyler.

The boy started to cry when he told us how sad he was that his father wouldn't be at his graduation from City College next year. He'd be graduating with honors. *Did I do this to that family? God, was it me?*

The boy's tears wracked his thin body, almost knocking him over. The priest gripped the boy by the elbow and guided him back to his seat like a blind man.

"The eulogy will be delivered today," the priest said, "by Harold Fielding, who worked very closely with Dan. Harry?"

"It's hard to explain what Dan meant to me," Harry began,

adjusting the tie that went with his blue suit. "We didn't see eye-to-eye on everything, but still he was a friend. One time I was flat broke. I hate to admit that, but I'd been drinking quite a lot and so . . . my career wasn't going so hot. I showed up in Dan's office one day, sober, but on the edge, and he gave me a job. That's why I'm standing here today. That job meant everything. It was a chance to rebuild my career. The career I have today. Now, I have a loving wife and a child . . ."

Harry took a handkerchief from his breast pocket and dabbed his eyes before continuing. "I will never forget him." He sat down.

The last to speak was the priest. He read from notes he'd prepared. It sounded like he'd never met Schuyler. He spoke about Schuyler's early troubles with the law and how he had completely turned his life around, so that up until the moment of his death he had been an upright citizen.

Upright citizen? What was the matter with everybody?

The priest led us in prayer for Schuyler's soul. Everything inside me beat to an uneven rhythm. I couldn't stop thinking that maybe Max had done this for me? Or for Jule? Or maybe it had been Mr. Wilferini, so he could take our clubs? Was I responsible for all this pain? I wanted to run right out of my own head.

As we stepped away from the coffin, men with umbrellas covered our heads and walked us to the cars.

"Uh, Max, that service," I said as I walked. "They made Schuyler out to be some kind of saint. You didn't . . .?"

"Al, please."

CHAPTER EIGHTEEN

"So this is where you come with Richard?" I put down my suitcase in the main room of the largest cabin I'd ever seen. "And others. You've brought others here too. Haven't you?"

"Let's not talk about others today. Okay?" She took off her apron. "This time is only for us." She wore a pair of black slacks and a pink-and-white striped cotton top with a pearl choker around her neck. "There are seven bedrooms in this place. We could sleep in a different one every hour if we wanted."

My eyes roamed over the wood-beamed ceiling that soared above us. There was a large dining table near the back wall of the room in front of the picture window. In the center of the room, there was a large sectional couch with end tables and lamps and such. A fireplace with partially burned logs sat not too far from the dining table.

"What's all that stuff by the stairs?" I asked. I walked over and pulled on the heavy canvas cover that seemed to be designed for hiding something.

Juliana removed my hand from the canvas and kissed it. "That's for later."

Across from the stairs was a small, upright piano.

"Tonight," I started, "could we sleep in one of the bedrooms you've never slept in with anyone?"

"Uh, well . . ."

"You mean there isn't even one? You've done it with someone in every single room? All seven of them?"

"Take it easy. I was only thinking. I know just the one. It'll be perfect for us. You go out and swim in the lake or walk around the grounds while I get it ready." She came close to me and pressed my cheeks between her thumb and forefinger. "You get the most precious pained look on you sometimes. I can't say I understand it, but—" She kissed my lips. "Now go. Give me time to get our room ready for tonight."

Our room. She said our room. The words rang through the huge evergreens above me. My God, they were big. I ran and skipped — yes, skipped. I hadn't skipped since I was seven. I skipped over the grass and it was green, oh, so green, all the way down to the wooden dock that stuck out into the lake. The whole way I repeated, "Our room, our room." Juliana and I had a room together. Both in one place. My heart was exploding. I breathed in the air. This weekend would be the best one in our whole lives. I walked onto the dock and listened to the water slosh against the posts that held the thing up. I took off my shoes and breathed; how lovely to be breathing, just breathing. No one was watching me, except of course, Juliana. I hoped. We were free. Free of Schuyler and . . . My heart slid down into my belly. I sat on the dock, my feet dangling over the side. Schuyler. Had I...? No, not today. I wouldn't let that man ruin today. I laid back on the dock, squinting into the sun, and drifted off into a pleasant sleep.

"Hey, you want to go for a swim?" Juliana said. I opened my eyes and saw her face staring down on me, like a sun. I sat up to see her better. She was wearing a knitted, white, loose-fitting cover-up over her bathing suit. "Go put your suit on and meet me down by the lake over there." She pointed in the direction she was heading. "We can take the row boat out."

"No kidding?"

"No kidding," she yelled back as she hurried down the slope to the boat that was beached there.

———

Juliana rowed the boat into the center of the lake. We were surrounded by mountains and tall evergreens, and I put Schuyler away and allowed my heart to soar. She rowed us into the center of the lake and pulled in the oars. She stood up, pulled her cover-up over her head, and threw it near my sneakered foot. She wore a white bathing suit with no skirt; it hugged her hips and breasts. I'd never seen her in a bathing suit before, but it was a beautiful sight. She stretched and got ready to dive over the side, while I lay back in my white terry cloth shirt and navy blue pedal pushers.

"Shall we?" she said. I pulled off my top, which covered my light blue bathing suit.

Before I could get my pedal pushers down my legs, Juliana, standing near the edge of the boat, pulled her suit down to her ankles.

"Jule! What are you doing?"

She stepped out of the suit. "Exactly what it looks like I'm doing. I'm going skinny dipping." She dove in and buoyed up to the surface. She pushed her wet hair off her forehead with both hands. "Your turn," she said. She looked like a boy with her hair slicked back like that, except, of course, for her lovely breasts floating near the top of the water. I could see her body gently moving in the soft current of the glass-clear lake. "Come on. Take your suit off."

"Are you out of your mind? What if someone sees us?"

"Who? The trees? They won't tell. Get that suit off."

I stepped out of my pedal pushers, folded them, and placed them on top of my terry cloth shirt. "This is as far as I go. I wasn't raised to go around doing things like that."

She laughed. "No matter what happens, you'll always be the little country girl. Come on, Country Girl, time to show what you've got. Take it off. Take it all off."

"You've already seen it." I dove in and came up next to her.

"Nice dive," she said, putting her arms around me. "How'd you learn?"

We held onto each other, treading water together. "In the summer when I was small, my father would take me to the ocean where there were lots of rocks, and we'd practice diving there."

"Lots of rocks? This wasn't so you'd knock yourself out, was it?"

"Of course not. The rocks weren't in the water. They were around it."

"Well, with *your* family, it's hard to know what the intention was."

"It was to teach me to dive. The crazy one was my mother. Not my father. Don't spoil my nice memory."

"Oh, honey." She hugged me. "I'm sorry."

"My mother would sit on the shore and watch. She wasn't always crazy."

"I know. I made a bad joke. I'm glad you have a nice memory. This is nice too. Being in the water with you and . . ." She pulled the straps of my bathing suit off my shoulders and down my arms.

"No!" I squealed, seeing the plan in her eyes; I swam away from her. She grabbed hold of my suit at the legs and pulled just as I took off. I swam right out of my suit. "Oh gosh, no." I slapped my arms over my chest.

She laughed and threw my bathing suit into the boat. "Now what are you going to do, Country Girl? If you go after it, all those trees are going to see you, and I hear the mountains are terrible gossips."

"Come on, Juliana, I feel so—well, so naked."

"*Really?* I can't imagine why?"

"Get it for me."

"Let me see you swim first."

"Then you'll get it?"

"I might."

"You are such a tease." I let go of my vice grip around my chest and swam freestyle away from her. She came up beside me. "Nice smooth strokes."

"I swim even better with clothes on."

"I doubt that." She turned onto her back. "Hey! You trees ever seen a rounder, firmer rear end than this one?"

We laughed and put our arms around each other and she touched my breasts. "Get a load of these sweet, little—"

"Yeah, little."

"Shut up. They're lovely." She kissed each one of my breasts. Then her fingers glided down the center of my body to between my legs.

"No Juliana, we can't . . . we can't . . ." She kept going and was turning me into her helpless jellyfish that might drown, but I didn't want her to stop—when . . . she did.

"No! Please." I looked at her face. "Oh, no, come on, Jule, you can't start that and then just—"

She backstroked toward the boat.

I swam after her. "Dammit, Jule!"

"Tonight, dear heart. Tonight."

———

We changed into short shorts and tops and dragged chaise lounges from the storage shed; we set them up on the front patio, so we could see the lake. We sat side by side, flipping through movie magazines. We had a pile of them sitting between us. It seemed like such a girly thing to do, and Juliana and I had never done girly things together. She looked lovely with her bare legs pushed into a triangle supporting the magazine.

"What do you think of this story in *Modern Screen?*" I asked.

"You mean the one about Rock Hudson being miserably lonely with his wife in Hollywood while he's in Rome shooting a picture?"

"Yeah. Isn't he . . .?"

"As a three-dollar bill, but only our people know it. They stick those silly articles in periodically to keep the public off the scent. I'm sure ol' Rock is making a few Italian boys very happy."

"Don't Debbie Reynolds and Eddie Fisher make an adorable couple?"

"Uh huh," Jule agreed.

"You can tell how in love they are by just looking at these pictures of them at home. I bet they stay together forever."

"Oh, Louella Parsons has a bit about that young kid, Sal Mineo, in here," Jule said. "He was terrific in *Rebel Without a Cause*. Louella liked him too. I hate when she tears up the kids. Bad for their confidence.

That whole movie had good young actors. It's a shame that new kid James Dean won't be able to have his career. A real loss."

"Yeah. There were a lot of tears for him at the Haven when we got the news. Louella covered Grace Kelly's wedding in here. When you were little did you ever dream of marrying a prince?"

"Heaven's no! I knew too many of them from my father's side of the family. Crashing bores. You?"

"No. I never dreamed about marrying anyone. Is this chaise lounge I'm sitting on Richard's?"

"Where did that come from out of the blue?"

"It is, isn't it?

"No, not Richard's. Mine."

"Then the one you're lying on is his?"

"Remember, we weren't going to do that while we're here. We have such a short time."

"Sorry. It's kind of a reflex. I have a confession to make."

"Do tell."

"Over the years, I've grown to like Richard."

"You're kidding."

"I've tried not to, but he's kind of an oddly likable fella. He's terrible with anything having to do with your career. He has no sense of theater or cabaret at all. But he's a good person. Easy to talk to, sometimes funny, caring, and he loves you to pieces. How could I not like a guy who feels like that?"

"I never expected that to come out of you."

"Me either. You know what's also weird? Despite liking him, I don't feel guilty about my relationship with you. I know I'm supposed to, but I can't manage it. It feels like they're just two different things, both important, but different. Is that how you fit him and me into your life?"

"I don't think I think things through as deeply as you do."

"Too bad we have to be secret about us with him. Sometimes I wish I could tell him how happy you make me and sometimes, I pretend that if he knew about us, it'd make him happy too."

"Well, pretending and reality *are* two very different things. I'm going to take a nap." She lowered the back of her chaise lounge.

"I'm going to join you in that nap." I stretched and lowered the back of my chaise lounge too.

I went in some in-between place with breezes lightly drifting over my body. The air grew cooler and I felt her hand on my arm. She whispered, "Let's have dinner."

———

While I slept, she'd made supper in the yellow kitchen behind a colorful curtain just a few steps beyond the main room. Instead of eating at the big dining table, we ate hotdogs and hamburgers at the little round table in the yellow kitchen.

"Oh, gosh, Jule, you can even make hamburgers taste out of this world."

"I didn't do anything special. Try a hotdog."

"I know you *did* do something special, because that's how you cook, but this . . ." I grabbed a hotdog from the plate in the center of the table where she'd put all the hotdogs in their buns. "I'd be five hundred pounds if you always cooked for me." I bit into the dog and fell back in my chair—ecstasy. "Oh, gosh, this is terrific too."

She laughed, flicking her napkin at me. "It's a hotdog."

"Not just any hotdog.It's almost as good as Nedick's."

"Almost?"

"No, better. It's even better than Nedick's. All that's missing is the Orangeade."

You're a little bit out of your mind, you know."

"Yeah, I do. Did you ever have a hope chest?" I asked as I devoured the rest of my hot dog.

Juliana put her hamburger down on her plate. "Yes. Yes, I did. I haven't thought about that in years. What made you think of that now?"

"Schuyler's coffin."

"What?"

"His coffin looked like my hope chest. Well, sorta. Mine was made of cedar chips, and I don't know why my hope chest popped into my mind in the church. Did you make a fuss about yours?"

"A little. When I was fourteen, I bought some pretty curtains that I imagined hanging in the kitchen I'd one day have." She got a faraway look. "I wonder what happened to them? Or the chest for that matter. Did you put special things in yours for the future?"

"Nah. My mother dreamed about the husband I'd marry, but *I* didn't. *She* put sheets and towels and pillowcases from when she was first married in there. She even put in her wedding dress, hoping one day I'd wear it. When it came time for me to wear one of those things, I was a lot skinnier than she had been, and the war was on and no one was wearing fancy wedding dresses anyway."

"But you still looked awfully pretty in yours."

"Yeah? You remember?"

"Of course. Do girls still keep hope chests?"

"I don't know. I don't know any young girls, but if I had a daughter, I wouldn't get her a hope chest."

"No?"

"No. I think she should decide for herself what she wants to do. I suppose most girls do get married, but not all of them."

"Obviously not. You didn't."

"But I'm an old maid. No girl wants to grow up to be that."

"Oh, stop."

"I think that's it."

"What?"

"Why I thought of my hope chest when I saw the coffin."

"Why?"

"Well, for me they're both about death."

"I don't know what to say to that. Except . . . you do the dishes." She wiped her mouth with her napkin and laid the napkin on the table.

"Oh?"

"Well, *I* cooked."

"True. Except I chopped the celery and carrots. Don't you have a dishwasher?"

"My goodness, no. Do you? Haven't you seen the prices they're getting on those?"

"Yeah, but you always have the latest thing and you never seem to worry much about cost, so I thought maybe . . ."

"But I don't want to be robbed. I would never spend that kind of money on a machine that does something I can easily do myself for free. We hardly ever come up here; it would be a waste. Are you really so opposed to dishwashing?"

"No. I just wanted to see how one works. I haven't seen one in person yet. Just in magazines."

"Do the dishes slowly." She rose from her seat. "I have things to do in the other room. Don't come out till I tell you."

———

As I put my hands into the soapy water, I knew I'd never been so happy in my whole entire life. *I didn't hurt Schuyler to have this.* I didn't cause *anything.* I didn't tell Mr. Wilferini to do that. That was true. Wasn't it? And now I was with her and she was out there doing "things" in the other room. Things to surprise *me. Oh, time stop here on this day.* Never move another notch forward. Let me live here always. There's no tomorrow. I'm in love. In love! I threw soap bubbles into the air.

Jule ran in.

"Ready?" I asked.

"Not yet. Put this on." She laid some clothes on a chair and ran back out.

It was the suit she'd made for me during the war. She'd saved it! I scrambled into it and stood on my side of the curtain. "Can I come out now? I need help with the tie."

"Yes! No! Wait. Just a minute."

She played the piano on the other side. I recognized the tune as one she'd sung in her first Copa act, "The Trouble with Me Is You." A fun song. It was on her first album.

"Okay," she called. "You can come out now."

I stepped into what she had transformed into a small nightclub. The lights were low and there was a round table with a white tablecloth in the center. A flickering candle and two wine glasses, not yet filled, sat on the table. A few feet away was a microphone and to the side, a hi-fi. Juliana wore a white satin dress that bounced around her silken calves; it had a low-cut bodice. She knew how much I liked peeking at her when she was fully clothed.

I walked toward her; she greeted me before I had reached the table. "First, let me fix that tie." Her fingers against my neck sent chills through my body.

"Okay, now you look gallant. Madame, welcome to the Chez Juliana," she said in a French accent. "Come." I followed her. "Mais bien sur, zee best seat in la maison."

I sat down, eager to be entertained by the sexiest, most glamorous, most talented night

club singer in the world, who was now even a Broadway star and would soon be a great opera diva.

She played records on the hi-fi while she danced and sang into the microphone, looking right at me. Neither of us concerned, at last, about who might be watching us. I even joined her in a few verses of the songs. Insisting we save the wine for later, she made us sidecars. I hadn't had a sidecar in almost a year. But here at Chez Juliana I could have them without worry. At the end of one of the songs, she stepped over to me at the table, poured white wine into each glass, picked up one of the glasses, and said, "To the most beautiful woman in the room."

"Me?" I said, standing, holding my own glass of wine.

"Mais bien sur, of course."

She clinked my glass and we took a sip. Then she took our glasses and put them on the table. She put her hand out. "May I have this dance?"

My heart beat in my throat like it did that first night. "Oh, yes, Jule, yes."

She lifted a delicate forefinger— "A minute"—and glided over to the hi-fi to remove the 33 rpm record. She replaced it with a 78. As the record began, she took me in her arms and sang "My Romance." The very first song she ever sang to me. The very first time she ever kissed me. We danced, swirling in an aura of our love like we were dancing in a timeless dream around and around.

"My romance doesn't have to have a moon in the sky," she sang.

"My romance doesn't need a blue lagoon standing by, no month of May . . ."

I wanted to shout, "I love you!" but I knew that would spoil it. She didn't want to hear that, and I was growing weary of saying it without it being returned. These moments, these wordless moments right now, these were the ones that had to be our moments. Nothing else could exist for us beyond now. But the song was coming to an end and I didn't want it to end. Cling to it. Stop it from ending. She sang:

"Wide awake I can make my most fantastic dreams come true."

And we stood still, looking deep into each other's eyes while she sang the last line, "My romance doesn't need a thing, but you."

She bent and kissed me. She kissed me long and deep and I wanted it to go on forever, but kisses always must end, and our lips parted.

Arms around each other, sleepy, we took our glasses of wine and walked to the top floor, to the bedroom she'd prepared. "Now, this room is not all that special," she said when we stood outside the door. "We use it for storage. That's where a lot of that hi-fi equipment came from. But it's a room that no one has ever slept in. It has a nice view. I just don't want you to be disappointed thinking it's some palatial suite. It's not; it's small and—"

I'd never known her to get anxious about pleasing me. "Can we go in?" I asked.

"Certainly, I just want you to know that it isn't—"

I pushed open the door. Inside was a canopy bed. The bedspread had a daisy pattern. It was a small room like she said, but warm. She'd spent all day making it warm. It smelled like wood. I walked over to the open window, where I could feel a light breeze. From there I could see the mountains and the trees, and the lake and a sky bursting with stars. "Oh, Jule." I held back my tears. She didn't like tears. "It's so beautiful."

"You like it?" She was practically hugging the doorjamb on the other side of the room as if afraid to enter. Afraid I wouldn't approve. "Yes, I like it. I like it very much."

She came over to me and put her hands on my shoulders. She turned me to face her and we kissed right in front of that window, as if our love was as good as anyone else's.

"I want to make love to you, Jule. However, you want it."

"*Really?*" she said with one of those glints in her eye that always warned me to be careful of what I promised. "It occurs to me that you owe me a strip tease."

"What?"

"I did it for you way back when. Now, it's your turn. I have a record player over there. I picked out some music."

"You sure thought of everything."

She put the record on the player and fixed it so it would keep playing over again. An instrumental song came on. "Bumps and Grinds" was the title.

"Where did you find something like this?"

"Oh, I get around." She picked up the fedora that sat on the dresser and put it on my head. "Wear this, doll face."

As the song continued to play with lots of booms and whistles, she sashayed to the bed and draped her lovely self across it, with her head and shoulders propped up with pillows. "Well?" She smiled and winked. "Take it off."

At first, I felt silly and awkward, but then I thought what the hell, and I just let the music take me over. I shimmied and shook and teased her to the music. I undid my tie and slid it off my neck real slow. I tossed it to her, and she caught it and kissed it. I twirled around and threw the fedora at her, then slowly opened each blouse button. Sometimes I pretended I was going to take something off, but then didn't. She oohed and aahed from the bed. A very appreciative audience. I slowly showed her one shoulder, then the other, but I couldn't help laughing. Neither could she. Finally, I took my shirt off and twirled it in the air, and she cheered. I let it go flying, and it landed somewhere. I teased her with unsnapping my bra. I threw the bra at her, and she caught it giggling like a teenager. Once my pants were down around my ankles, I climbed into the bed and into her arms. She finished taking off my pants. "I'd better turn off that grinding music or we're both going to end up certifiable," I said.

I got up to turn off the music and when I turned around, she was stepping out of her dress. I watched as she took everything off and covered herself in a semi-sheer nightgown. We lay in each other's arms, staring out at the night sky. "I hardly believe this is real," I said. "You and me lying here. The only outside world is that sky."

Juliana sighed. "It's good, isn't it?"

I wanted to say "I love you," but I didn't want to make her uncomfortable, so I let my heart say it to her heart.

She ran her hand over my breasts down to the waistband of my underpants. She slowly pushed them down while she kissed me. My hand found its way past her nightgown to the curve of her hip and down her thigh. She sighed and slid down onto her back. She reached into the top drawer of the end table. "Do you mind?"

A dildo and harness lay there. "I'd love to."

I kissed her breasts, her belly, her clit. Then, at the right time, I cinched myself into the dildo.

By the time we'd gotten into bed, there wasn't much left of the night. We were sleepy, but still not satiated, when the stars began to fade. I pulled her close to me. I didn't want those stars to go. I didn't want to move on into this day of separation, of back to business, of back to pretending. We were something different here.

Suddenly, I was seized with the heat of her. I had to possess her. Possess her more than I ever had. Never let her go. Time was ticking away. Our time was going. I got on top of her and pushed the dildo deep inside her. She gasped. I touched her clit and kissed her breasts and moved up and down on her, anything I could do to have her in me and me in her. We were one. Forget the world.

She threw her arms around my neck and we moved together. Merging, merging into one.

I had to have her in me. She was yelling, "Yes! Yes! More! Please, more, Al, I need, I need . . ." At the highest point, when I knew she was climaxing, she yelled out, "I love you, Al!"

I stared into her face for just a moment until she melted into the bed sheets and turned her head away. We were still connected, and I was afraid to move. Afraid to go into those next few seconds. We must stay here with more than a piece of rubber connecting us. We must stay here, not talking. I was content to listen to her breath and replay that moment, that moment I thought I didn't imagine, that moment I thought was real, that moment she said, "I love you, Al."

"Uh, so, Al," she said, giving me a light push off of her. The next moment had come and we were separating. I watched from the bed as she got up and put on her robe. "I'll make breakfast."

She never turned to look back at me.

I reached out and touched her hand. "Jule."

"Breakfast," she repeated, still not turning, and padded out of the room without her slippers.

I saw that she had brought my suitcase into this room. It lay against the wall near the Victrola. I put on a pair of trousers, a shirt, and sneakers and went down the stairs to the kitchen. She had a pot of coffee going and was standing over the burner, swishing around the scrambled eggs. "I hope scrambled is okay." She didn't turn to see me.

"Sure. Terrific."

"I made coffee instead of tea, because I love the smell of coffee in the morning. I can make tea if you prefer."

"No. I like coffee in the morning."

"I know so little about you," she said softly, pushing the eggs onto two plates with the spatula. She brought them to the table. "I should've made bacon. I forgot. How did I ever forget? I have it, but I didn't— I can make it now."

"No. This is fine. I'm not that hungry anyway."

"Yes. So what else do I need to, to, uh . . ." She looked around the kitchen, everywhere but at me.

"I'll get the coffee," I said.

"No, I'll get it." She poured coffee into two cups and brought them to the table. "I forgot the saucers. What's wrong with me?" She went to the cupboard to get the saucers and her hands shook. She dropped one and it smashed to the floor. "*Now* look what I've done."

I jumped up. "Careful. You're not wearing anything on your feet." I took the other saucer from her hand. "I've got it. Sit down. I'll get the dustpan and broom."

"They're here." She lifted them from behind the refrigerator. "I can do it."

"You don't have slippers on. Let me. You sit."

She let me take the broom and dustpan from her limp grip, but she didn't sit. She stood there, as if not sure what she should be doing. I put the intact saucer under her cup and got a second one for me. "Jule, sit. Your bare feet are making me a wreck. Sit. I'll be done in a minute."

As I dumped the pieces into the garbage, she unfolded her linen napkin and laid it across her lap. I joined her, ready to eat. "It's cold," she said. "You can't eat that. I'll make new."

She was about to swipe my plate out from under my fork when I grabbed her arm. "I'm not all that interested in food right now."

"Oh?" She began to eat her own eggs at a feverish pace. "Al, things — things happen—there are reflexes—when one is, one is, in certain, certain conditions and . . . I can't eat these." She got up and tossed her eggs in the trash.

I stood and put an arm around her. "Jule. It's okay." She laid her head on my shoulder and I stroked her hair. "Shh, Jule, shh."

"Oh, Al, what am I going to do?"

"We'll figure something out. Together."

CHAPTER NINETEEN

I hurried toward Carnegie Studios. A messenger had arrived at the Haven on his bicycle with a note for me. He looked like Elvis Presley with his hair cut in that new style they were calling a DA. DA stands for duck's ass, so I'm not sure why anyone would want their hair cut like that, except—I was kinda getting to like it myself, and even started picturing how it would look on me, which of course was one of my more ridiculous thoughts. Women couldn't wear their hair that way. But I had seen a couple of women in the street with hair like that, the obvious gay girls. But I couldn't walk around that way and expect to keep my job. Max thought kids like my messenger just needed a haircut.

My young messenger almost missed me. I was carrying out a large bag of laundry on my shoulders, some of it from my time in the mountains with Juliana earlier in the week. I always brought my laundry to the Haven so in between things, I could stop off at the self-service laundromat. I was never home long enough to do it there. Once the note from Jule landed in my hand, I dropped the laundry at the door with Giorgio and took off. How wonderful to be summoned by messenger to Juliana's side. It meant she was clear to see me. All my chores, my laundry, my grocery shopping, everything could wait.

Juliana beckoned. She said Studio 330. We'd never been in that studio before, but Jule had a flare for the mysterious.

It'd been hard leaving her Monday morning. But we had begun talking about using the cabin as our retreat on a regular basis. Maybe every couple of months or so we could go there. That was probably all we could hope for now, but in the future . . . Who knew? Juliana loved me. She said it out loud. And she didn't take it back. She even told me she wasn't seeing any other girls. I didn't ask her; she told me on her own. She said she wasn't going to see any other girls anymore. All was right with the world. I got through the next few days of running the Haven by replaying everything we'd done together in my mind. That was some day and a half! Especially that night. I'd close my eyes and bring back the scene and hear her crying out, "I love you, Al!" Just picturing it made vibrating thrills run up and down my body.

Earlier in the week, I'd gotten a call from the producer of the opera Juliana had auditioned for back in June. They loved her and wanted to hire her! The contracts were sent to Richard, of course, and he and Juliana signed them. But *I* was the one who had made all the arrangements. She would finish out the run of *Heaven is to Your Left* and begin rehearsals for the opera soon after. It still didn't have a title. Juliana must be ecstatic to be finally signed to an opera. She was pleasing her mother at last. I thought she might call me as soon as she got the contract, but she hadn't. That must be why she arranged for us to meet today.

The day was pleasantly cool, and it was before noon, so the sidewalks weren't too crowded. I loved walking in the city on a day like this. I felt light and airy. Juliana lived deep inside me, and I could feel her breathing there. She loves me, she loves me, she loves me.

I bounced into the elevator at the Carnegie Studios and the elevator operator nodded at me. "Morning, ma'am."

"Yes. Yes, it is a very good morning, indeed. My name's Al."

"Al?"

He got that scrunched up look that people get when I tell them my name without giving them the formal one. "Oh. Sorry. Alice. What's yours?"

"Stephen, ma'am." He was a slim young man and looked fit in his brown uniform.

"Well, it's very nice to meet you, Stephen." I extended my hand.

He looked at my hand like he wasn't sure what to do with it. Then he shrugged his

shoulders in a "what the heck gesture" and took my fingers lightly in his. "Likewise, I'm sure, ma'am. Floor?"

"Oh, yes, of course." I laughed. "You need to know that before you can take me there, don't you?"

"Yes, ma'am," he said, laughing with me.

"Then onward to floor three, young Stephen."

"Nonstop, ma'am."

When he opened the door on the third floor I felt a slight pang of sadness, like I was leaving a friend. From the way he looked at me, I sensed he felt the same. "Well, ma'am, you have yourself a wonderful day."

"I will, I will," I said. "And you do the same.

"Thank you. I'll be sure to do that." He said it like he was making a personal promise to me. Too bad I was never allowed to share with people how much in love I was.

I found the door to room 330 and pushed through. It was a small room, smaller than Juliana ever used for rehearsal. It had a piano and some wooden folding chairs, but no stage. It was a rather dreary looking room. Just a few dirty windows over a dormant radiator.

"Al," Juliana's voice came from the doorway behind me. I jumped, not expecting she'd be there so soon. The elevator had just left.

"I was waiting in the hallway. I arrived a little early."

"Oh." She looked lovely in her red polka-dotted day dress with the white trim around the collar and the short sleeves. She wore a small round hat on her head and carried a red and white box purse. No gloves.

I rushed toward her, then stopped, remembering we couldn't embrace, but aching to feel her in my arms. "Morning," I said. I could feel the big goofy grin on my face.

"Good morning," she returned, but *her* face did not have morning in it. Something was wrong.

"What is it?"

"Uh, well . . ." She walked fully into the room, closing the door behind her. "Uh...I don't know how to . . ." She walked to the corner near the radiator and opened her handbag removing a package of filtered Lucky Strikes.

"What?" I said, the blood in my veins rushing to my head at panic speed. "What's happened?"

She lit a Lucky and took a puff.

"Why are we here? What's wrong?" I hammered at her.

"I — I wanted to meet with you where there was very little chance that anyone would question us being together. You know a rehearsal studio?" Her voice shook. "Let me try to say this without you interrupting me. I have to get it out quickly."

I held my breath.

"Richard." She took another puff of her cigarette. "He . . . Well, he . . . knows about us."

"What?" Had my heart stopped?

"Please. Don't say anything. This—this is hard. He suspected that I was having an affair with Max—where he ever got such a crazy idea I can't fathom except— he's always accusing me—These men. He thinks there are these men . . .There are no men!—so when I planned to go away to Maine . . ." She paced, quickly putting the cigarette in her mouth and out again. "I've been there hundreds of times without him. Why, oh, why this time did he have to . . .! He had me followed. A private detective." She stopped pacing and took a long puff from the cigarette.

"What does this mean?" I asked.

"I, uh, can't . . .we can't . . . see . . . uh, see each other." She sucked back a tear that was trying to get out.

"No! That's wrong. We'll go away somewhere. We can't let him—"

"Where would we go? Talk sense, Al. Even if we both gave up our careers, how would we live? What place would receive people like us?"

"No! No!" This time *I* paced up and down, my hands over my ears.

"Al." She held out a shaking hand toward me.

I hurried to her, taking her hand in mine.

"No." She pulled her hand away. "We mustn't. We must never . . ."

She walked away, taking a few quick puffs from her cigarette. "Richard was so enraged, shocked. I've never seen him so upset. I thought he was going to hit me."

"He didn't?"

"No. But if I don't stop seeing you, he'll divorce me in a most public and humiliating manner. He'll call you in as correspondent. There are pictures."

"Pictures."

"Both of our lives would be ruined."

"I don't care."

"Al, you say that now, but . . . He would get his divorce and my house, and everything I own. I would have nothing."

"I have money. We could, could . . ."

"Where would you work once this got out? Max would have to let you go or he'd lose everything too. What would that accomplish? Now is the time for you to think with your head, not with your heart, oh dear, sweet one. I have to go. Richard is downstairs waiting. He won't wait long." She moved toward the door.

"No!" I ran to block her exit. "You can't let him do this to us, Jule. There's a way. We just need to think and plan. I have a teaching degree! I can—"

"What school would let you near children once they knew about this?"

"Well, there's another way. There's got to be some way. There has to be! Please, Jule!"

"Al!" she yelled. "Stop it! Stop holding on to some impossible dream." Tears now streamed from her eyes and she didn't try to stop them. "I have to go." She made a step to move past me, and I blocked her again.

My own tears poured. "Gertrude Stein and Alice B. Toklas. People accepted them. We'd be like them."

She sighed, wiping her tears with a handkerchief. "That was Paris. In the 1920s. The world's not there, anymore. Not even Paris."

"You love me. I know you do. You *know* you do."

"My feelings have . . . have nothing . . . to do with this." She could barely get the words out. "Please don't make this uglier than it already is. I have no choice. *We* have no choice." She moved toward the elevator, and I ran in the hallway after her. She pushed the buzzer.

"Who the hell got you that opera? You know Richard didn't do it. You know he could *never* do it. He didn't do anything for your career. It was me. All me. I got you your whole career."

"I'll have the elevator operator come up for you after I'm down."

"Stephen! His name is Stephen! You promised no one would see us in those mountains.

You promised, Jule."

The elevator door opened. As she stepped inside, I yelled, "I hate you. I hate you. I hate you. I'll always hate you." The door slid closed and Stephen took her away from me.

End of Book 4

ALSO BY VANDA WRITER

Want to Know What Happens Next?

Get Your Free Excerpt from Book 5
(as of this writing not yet published)

LINK TO YOUR FREE EXCERPT BELOW

https://dl.bookfunnel.com/5gmab9j2g8

YOUR OPINION COUNTS

Dear Reader,

Your opinion matters to me and it matters to other readers. Your reviews make me a better writer.

I hope you'll leave a review of this book or any of the others you've read. A review can be short or long; I prize them all.

Leave your review here
My Book

The Juliana Series

Be Sure You Read the Whole Series
Click Below
My Book

ACKNOWLEDGEMENTS

Some Very Important Thank You's

Phillip Crawford, Jr., author of *The Mafia and The Gays* and *Railroaded*, two books I recommend, was my vitally important adviser and teacher about the workings of the mob. I am so very grateful for his help. Without him I would not have been able to achieve the accuracy I shoot for in all my books.

I am also very grateful to my Beta readers, Sallie Castillo and Eileen Howell, who read an earlier draft of *Heaven it to the Left* and gave their honest feedback.

I also want to thank the readers on my newsletter list and my street team who offer their support and their ideas.

ABOUT VANDA

I was born and raised in Huntington Station, New York. This town shouldn't be confused with Al's home town of Huntington. They are two different towns, and it's too long a story to explain the significance of that difference. Now, I live in New York City, and I have for quite some time. I've been a professor at Metropolitan College of New York for over fifteen years, but I don't teach writing like many people guess. I teach psychology because my advanced training is in psychology, and I am a licensed psychologist.

I was a writer long before I was a psychologist. I wrote my very first novel in eighth grade with encouragement from my teacher, Mr. James Evers, who would meet me before school every week to discuss the latest pages I had penned. He wrote in my junior high yearbook, "My children will read your words." Unfortunately, others were not quite so encouraging, and I wandered away from my writing. I spent a lot of years going from job to job because the work-a-day world could not satisfy a restlessness in my soul. Along the way, I found playwriting and was a playwright for about twenty years. The desire to tell the story of LGBT history with fictional characters who live through that history brought me back to my original form, the novel, but I learned a lot about dialogue from playwriting.

I'd love to hear from you. My online home is www.vandawriter.com. Come sign up for my mailing list there and get info about new releases and forthcoming events. You can also connect with me on Goodreads at https://www.goodreads.com/drvanda or on Facebook at https//www.facebook.com/vandawriter or www.twitter @vandawriter. You can contact me directly at vanda@vandawriter.com

 facebook.com/vandawriter

 twitter.com/drvanda

instagram.com/vdrvanda

NOTES

7. MARCH 1956

1. Dr. Murray Banks was a psychology professor at Long Island University, Pace College and Brooklyn College. He was a popular speaker for men's and women clubs and conventions. The lecture depicted here comes from a 33 rpm record album, entitled, "What You Can Learn from the Kinsey Report.

CHAPTER 15

1. *Shane,* the movie was released in 1953. Its most famous and haunting line, yelled out by Joey, a small farm boy, is "Shane! Come back!" Alan Ladd is known for transforming "the gangster with his ugly face, gaudy cars and flashy clothes (into) "a smoother, better looking, better dressed killer."